the year money grew on trees

written and illustrated by
Aaron Hawkins

sandpiper

Houghton Mifflin Harcourt
Boston   New York

The text of this book is set in Bembo.
The illustrations were created using pen and ink.

The Library of Congress has cataloged the hardcover edition as follows:
Hawkins, Aaron R.
The year money grew on trees / written and illustrated by Aaron R. Hawkins.
p. cm.
Summary: In early 1980s New Mexico, thirteen-year-old Jackson Jones recruits his
cousins and sisters to help tend an elderly neighbor's neglected apple orchard for the
chance to make big money and, perhaps, to own the orchard.
[1. Apple growers—Fiction. 2. Farm life—New Mexico—Fiction.
3. Cousins—Fiction. 4. Brothers and sisters—Fiction. 5. Moneymaking projects—
Fiction. 6. New Mexico—History—20th century—Fiction.] I. Title.
PZ7.H31347Ye 2010
[Fic]—dc22
2009049703

ISBN: 978-0-547-27977-0 hardcover
ISBN: 978-0-547-57716-6 paperback

Manufactured in the United States of America
DOC 10 9 8 7 6 5 4 3 2

4500348959

To Jackrabbit for getting me started
and Kellie for getting me finished

CONTENTS

← To
Shiprock

U.S. Highway 550

Dirt
Road

X

Mrs.
Nelson's
House

To
Farmington →

The
Orchard

Jackson's
House

Amy's
House

Chapter 1
A BAD CHOICE AND A WORSE ONE

My dad always said that his feet were the only stupid parts of his body. They had walked him into every bad decision he had ever made, so he had to watch them carefully. He repeated that little pearl of wisdom so often that I began to take it literally and stare at my feet when they were moving. I had my eyes on them the afternoon they walked me into my career in agriculture. I blame my feet because I was only thirteen at the time and not exactly in the job market.

On that particular day, I was mostly thinking about what I could eat when I got home from school. I was trudging along the dirt lane from the bus stop while my sisters and cousins rushed past me, trying to escape the biting New Mexico wind. The lane's rutted tracks had filled with water from a snowstorm and then frozen into narrow strips of dirty ice. It felt powerful and satisfying to crush the fragile surfaces and watch the underlying brown water ooze around my shoes. I was careful to find and eliminate each of the thin ice plates that had survived the weak February sun. I imagined it sounded a little like breaking glass. *Crunch, crack, crunch, SLAM!*

My head shot up at the familiar sound of a screen door banging against a door frame. I had made it far enough down the lane so that I was next to the house of my neighbor Mrs. Nelson. I looked up with a guilty face, expecting to be accused of some crime involving ice breaking. Instead of Mrs. Nelson coming toward me down her walk, however, it was her grown son, Tommy. I could tell right away he was mad. His face was puckered and red, and his fists were clenched, ready to hit something. As he got closer, I dropped my eyes and concentrated on my feet, even though they had stopped moving. I heard a car door opening and then slamming shut, followed by the gunning of an engine as Tommy turned his car onto the dirt road. I jumped toward Mrs. Nelson's to avoid Tommy's front grille, and little pieces of gravel flew up against my leg as the car roared by. Tommy didn't even turn his head to acknowledge me.

As I stood watching the car disappear, Mrs. Nelson's head popped out of the screen door. "Is he gone?" she yelled.

"Yeah!" I yelled back a little too loudly, given that we were only fifty feet apart.

"Did he say anything to you, Jackson?" she asked a little quieter as she stepped off her porch toward me.

"No. But he almost ran me over," I answered dramatically.

She stared at me, her eyes moving from my wet shoes to my ears, which were turning red from being stared at and because of the subfreezing temperature. "Why don't you come in for a minute?" she finally said, motioning toward her door.

I'd talked with Mrs. Nelson hundreds of times on her porch and outside her house, but she'd never invited me in before. A small tingle of fear ran down my back for some reason.

"Okay. I probably can for a minute."

On the way toward the porch, I remembered my muddy shoes. I tried to slide along the dead grass next to Mrs. Nelson's walkway to scrape off some of the mud. I spent several moments dragging my shoes across the WELCOME, FRIENDS mat she had in front of her door. She finally said, "That's enough. Now come in before we heat up the whole outdoors."

I hesitated inside the doorway, unsure whether to take

off my shoes, but she motioned to a chair in her front room as if I was supposed to sit down. I slinked over, glad that the carpet was off-brown. The room itself was very neat, but with lots of little shelves and cabinets full of things my dad would call worthless clutter—snow globes from all fifty states, statues of fat little angels, and shiny bowls and glasses in pale pinks and greens.

Before I knew it, Mrs. Nelson was handing me a cup of cocoa. It was just cool enough that I could tell it had been made way before my arrival. "How's your family doing? How's your mother?" she asked, sitting across from me.

She had never asked about my family before, and I took my first good look at her. The way she was dressed reminded me a little bit of her house—neat but with too many fancy accessories for someone who lived down a dirt road. She had probably spent an hour arranging her graying hair but it had unraveled, and I could see by her eyes she had been crying. "My mom's okay," I managed to squeak out.

"You need to always remember your mother and how much she does for you, even when you get older."

"Uh-huh," I mumbled, as I pretended to be interested in the cocoa.

"Because what really matters in this life is your family, and you always have to treat them right." Mrs. Nelson paused a few seconds and looked around the room.

"You know, it's all been so different since my husband died. You'd think being alone like I am, Tommy would be happy to spend time with me."

The way Mrs. Nelson was talking reminded me of something, and when she reached her last sentence, I knew what it was. She sounded just like my mom after she and my dad had been arguing. I knew right then that I was supposed to nod my head a lot and agree with her. Tell her things like "He just doesn't appreciate you" and "You deserve better." I started the head nodding and was about to say something sympathetic when she continued.

"And now my doctor says I might have cancer, and my own son acts like he doesn't even care. Tells me I'm being overdramatic." Mrs. Nelson reached for a tissue and dabbed at her eyes.

Awkwardness filled up the room and pushed my shoulders to the floor. I could tell Mrs. Nelson was waiting for some kind of response, but I had no idea what to say. I looked down at my cocoa and then managed, "I'm sorry."

"Wouldn't you want to spend more time with your mother if she only had a year to live?" asked Mrs. Nelson in a voice dripping in self-pity.

I squirmed nervously in my chair. "Yeah, I would," I replied weakly, and nodded my head.

"I've even asked him to help with my will, but he

doesn't care about that either. Says I should just sell this house and all the land around it. Acts like he hates it out here."

There was a long pause that signaled my turn to say something. "Maybe he just likes living in town. My mom always wishes she did." It was the most profound thing I could think of.

"Tommy's father would roll over in his grave if he heard that. He moved us out here to get away from the city. Planted that orchard in front because he wanted to act like a farmer. It almost kills me to look at it now in a shambles."

Between Mrs. Nelson's house and the road was an apple orchard that had been abandoned since Mr. Nelson had died. Since as far back as I could remember, it had been a part of my landscape, but mostly off-limits according to my mom.

Mrs. Nelson sat up straighter in her chair, and her voice got a little higher. "Oh, he loved being in that orchard. He always said there was something about being close to the earth that was spiritual and primal. I always loved those blossoms breaking out in the spring. I'm always begging Tommy to get it going again, put some water on the trees at least."

I kept nodding my head and trying to seem interested.

"You know, when Tommy was about your age, his father tried to get him to help out with those trees, but he was always happier doing something else, anything else." She shook her head. "How old are you now, Jackson? Fourteen, fifteen?"

"I'll be fourteen in a few weeks," I mumbled.

"In a lot of ways, you remind me more of my husband than Tommy does. The way you always like to be outside and working with your hands."

I gave her a halfhearted grin to acknowledge the compliment. Being outside all the time was mostly due to my mother's policy on not overcrowding the house rather than a conscious personal choice. As for working with my hands, Mrs. Nelson was probably referring to all her yard work she had cornered me into doing. She looked above my head like she was trying to see something off in the distance. Then she began talking quietly to herself as if I weren't in the room.

"I just hate to see it neglected like that. It breaks my heart to think that Tommy would just dig up those trees. Probably put a trailer park over it or something. Serve him right if I gave it to someone who'd keep it up." All of a sudden she lowered her eyes and stared me into blushing. "How about you? How'd you like that orchard?"

"Uh . . . m-me? What would I do with it?"

"Raise apples, of course. That's the whole point. If you do it right, you can make plenty of money too."

That last part caught my attention, and I sat up a little

straighter. "But why me? I don't know anything about apples."

"I just need someone willing to learn. Someone who can prove they'll take care of the place when I'm gone."

"How would I prove that?"

Mrs. Nelson leaned back like she was thinking. "You could work on it this year and give me a chance to examine the results. Then I'll decide."

The idea of her giving me the orchard sounded pretty meaningless to thirteen-year-old ears. Why would I want the thing? The interesting part in what she was saying was the possibility of making some money. "What about the money, if, you know, there were some apples that were sold?"

Mrs. Nelson got a distasteful look on her face. "Money. Well, yes, I guess you could have some of the money, depending on what kind of job you did. The same kind of arrangement we make when you work in my yard."

My heart sunk. The "arrangement" we had with her yard was that she would promise me $5 for something that supposedly took only a couple of hours. After an entire Saturday of breaking my back for her, she'd hand me a dollar bill and say my work wasn't up to $5 standards. Once she even sent me home without the usual dollar because I pulled up hydrangeas I thought were weeds. She'd screeched like I'd killed a bunch of puppies.

I'd never learned to say no, however, and gotten suckered into the same thing dozens of times. The orchard sounded like an even bigger con job. I'd probably work every day for a year, make her a bunch of money, and then she'd hand me a dollar bill. "Not up to $5 standards," she'd say. "And I'm giving the orchard to someone else now that it's all cleaned up." I looked down at my feet and didn't say anything.

"What do you think? You willing to take over for my husband? Make those trees come alive again?" Mrs. Nelson asked insistently.

"I'll have to think about it," I replied slowly. That was the answer my dad gave to all salesmen. He said that was standard practice no matter how much you wanted something or how good the deal seemed. This deal didn't seem that good, and I really would have to think about it.

"Think about it?" asked Mrs. Nelson, acting very put out. "Well, don't think too long. Opportunities like this come along once in a lifetime. People don't just go around giving away land and orchards."

I thanked her for the cocoa and got up to leave. I remembered to tell her I was sorry to hear about the cancer and hoped she felt better. After a few sighs and dramatic sniffles, she walked me to the door. "I expect to hear back from you right away about the orchard," she called as I hurried around the corner of her house.

When I walked in my front door, my mom didn't seem to notice it had taken me an extra long time to return from the bus stop. I didn't dare mention the orchard proposition to her or to my dad when he got home. They had always seemed to avoid and distrust Mrs. Nelson. Somehow she had singled me out as the one person in our family she would talk to, but only if she caught me walking along the dirt road past her house. Since I knew her better than anyone and I'd be doing all the work, I felt like I could make a decision about the orchard on my own. The idea made me feel anxious but grown-up. By the time dinner rolled around, I had convinced myself that the smartest thing to do was to ignore Mrs. Nelson and let her plan fade away. It seemed like just a crazy impulse she'd had, anyway.

My family sat down to eat with my mom and dad at either end of the table and my two little sisters sitting across from me. Dad had on the usual worn-down expression he wore after work, and he was still wearing his denim work shirt. My mom pointed out two of his favorite dishes—scalloped potatoes and pot roast—and then began cheerfully filling up plates. Dad grunted his appreciation.

"I stopped by the scrap yard on the way home," Dad announced after taking a few bites. "Talked with ol' Slim Nickles. He says he gets really busy during the summer and needs extra help. Just manual labor kinds of things, no skills required. I told him I had a son who didn't have any skills but could probably haul things around. Slim said we could stop by and he'd look you over." Dad finished by pointing his fork at me.

I let my fork drop on my plate and my mouth hang open. The scrap yard was on the side of the highway Dad took to work, and he loved stopping in and searching through the mounds of metallic junk. He'd stop in on Saturdays, too, and drag me along. I couldn't stand the place. It was filthy and smelled like burning rubber. And Slim Nickles was the biggest jerk I'd ever met. He was usually covered in grease and had a wide red face and a huge gut. He yelled every word he said and loved to intimidate people. The one time he'd noticed me, he warned me to keep my hands in my pockets or he'd snap them off.

Before any sounds of protest could come from my mouth, Mom spoke up. "He's only thirteen. Are you sure he's old enough to have a job?"

"He'll be fourteen this summer. When I was fourteen, I was working as much as a grown man, maybe more," replied Dad, his voice getting louder.

Mom rolled her eyes. "Are you sure that's going to be a safe place for a boy to work?"

"It'll be safe enough. As long as he's not just sitting around the house like last summer. Any more of that and he'll be a freeloader the rest of his life."

"Oh, Dan," Mom said. "Don't sound so mean. You're going to give your own son a complex."

"I'm just trying to do what's best for him. My dad never let me just lay around."

"I'd be happy to have a job," I broke in, "but does it have to be at the scrap yard?"

"I don't care where it is, but you'll have to find someone who'll hire a fourteen-year-old. Slim's the only one I know."

The orchard popped into my head, but I didn't want to say anything about it. My mind raced through other potential employers anywhere near my house. "What about that snow-cone stand by the school?"

"That guy's got all his kids working there. Nah, this weekend we'll go talk to Slim and get things lined up."

I stayed quiet the rest of dinner, stewing about the scrap yard. If I put up a big fight and refused to go, my dad would make life at home miserable. And if I went along with him, Slim would be more than happy to make my time away from home miserable. Either way, I was bound to be miserable. I had to find something else, almost anything else.

Chapter 2
SAVED FROM THE SCRAP YARD

In only a matter of hours, my life had accelerated un-controllably. My only worries had been homework and girls, but all that seemed in the distant past. My future depended on a choice between two terrible jobs I didn't need. I realized I didn't want to feel grown-up anymore.

I hadn't decided anything until lunch at school the next day. I watched Slim's son Skeeter cut in the caf-eteria line and then punch the kid behind him who protested. Skeeter was a grade ahead of me but a couple of years older. He was built like his dad and maybe even meaner. The proudest moment of his life was when he made a substitute teacher run out of his class crying. While the sub was gone, Skeeter lit the garbage can on fire and then peed it out, bragging he was "saving the class."

I stared at Skeeter and realized he'd be at the scrap yard all summer too. Maybe he'd even be my boss. That afternoon I knocked on Mrs. Nelson's door right after getting off the bus.

"Ah, Jackson. I thought you'd be back," she said when she answered the door. "Why don't you come in again?"

I shuffled over to the same chair I'd sat in the day before. Mrs. Nelson sat across from me again looking more composed. The tears were gone and all her hair was neatly in place.

"I've been thinking about the orchard," I began, "and I think I'd like to do it. There's just one little thing."

"Oh? What's that?"

"Could we maybe agree on a way to split the money from the apples? Say, you get a certain percentage and I get a certain percentage?"

"You're still worried about the money, are you? Remember, that's not what's important to me. I could just go hire anyone off the street if I wanted to make money. After you left yesterday, I realized I was really looking for the orchard's true heir." She said that last sentence as if she were reading from a book of fairy tales.

I wasn't sure what to say about the "true heir" stuff.

All I wanted was to get some number or percentage out of her mouth. "I promise to work super hard. But maybe if I had a goal to shoot for, it would help keep me going."

"I told you I'd take care of you. You'll get rewarded according to how you work."

"Yes, but if there was just something specific, I think it would be better. You know, if I do this and this, then you do that."

"Ah, don't you trust me? Think I'm not really serious?"

"No, it's not that—it's just . . ."

"Fine. Let's be specific," she said, cutting me off. "You get that orchard running and pay me a certain amount, and then you can have the rest of the money and more importantly the orchard."

"Okay," I said cautiously, "how much?"

"Let's see," she said with a look of disgust on her face, as if the very thought of money was repulsive. "From what I remember my husband making, I'd say $8,000 would be about right."

"Eight thousand dollars? That's impossible!" I gasped almost involuntarily. I hadn't imagined making even a tenth of that.

"Impossible? You're thinking like a child. There are 300 trees out there. They'll each produce several bushels, and at the grocery store a bushel of apples is $25 or more.

That's a lot more than $8,000. It's practically like grow-
ing money on trees."

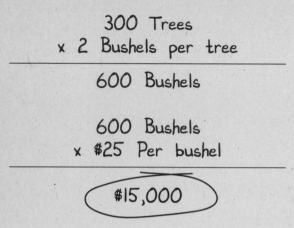

300 Trees
x 2 Bushels per tree
─────────────────
600 Bushels

600 Bushels
x $25 Per bushel
─────────────────
$15,000

I roughly did the math in my head; and it came out
to almost twice $8,000. I wasn't 100 percent sure of her
or my math, but if the numbers were right, I'd make
plenty of money plus whatever the orchard was worth.
"It would be a lot of work, though," I finally said.

"It's supposed to be. I'm looking for the true heir, remember. If you do that much work, I'm sure you'll want
to keep watching over those trees."

There she went with the "true heir" stuff again. It still
sounded like there was a good chance I wouldn't get
anything. "I don't understand why we can't just split the

money, and then you can decide whether you want to give me the orchard or not."

"It doesn't matter if you don't understand. I understand and it's my orchard and I'm going to do what's best for it." Her voice got higher and took on a tone that meant I shouldn't argue. I could tell I was getting pushed around, but I had nowhere else to go.

"I guess it will be all right, then," I said quietly. "I'll just have to make that $8,000 somehow." I was mostly talking to myself, trying to quiet all the doubts raging through my head.

"We're agreed, then," Mrs. Nelson said, smiling for the first time.

"Shall we shake hands on it or something?" I asked sheepishly.

"I've got a better idea. Let's put it in writing. I've got a lawyer in town working on my will. We'll have him write something up. I told Tommy about our plan this morning, and he said I'd never do it. I can't wait to show him a written contract." A vindictive grin spread over her face. "We can still get there before the lawyer leaves for the day."

"Now? Go now?"

"Yes, now. Let me get my coat."

Mrs. Nelson stood up and I followed her. "Let me just run home and tell my mom," I said, a little dazed.

"Right, right. I'll meet you out at my car."

Mrs. Nelson didn't seem like the type of person to do things on the spur of the moment, so it was surprising to see how determined she was to act immediately. I wasn't about to argue, however, so I ran home and found my mom. She was talking on the phone, but I cut in.

"Mrs. Nelson needs me to go to Farmington with her. Needs some help with something," I said, out of breath.

Mom excused herself on the phone and then looked at me suspiciously. "What kind of help?"

"I dunno. Didn't really say."

"Okay. But you behave yourself." She gave me an annoyed look and went back to her phone call.

I could tell she wanted to say I couldn't go but couldn't think of a good-enough reason.

"Let's go before it gets too late," called Mrs. Nelson from inside her car as I walked up.

I got in the front seat. Mrs. Nelson had a 1982 Caprice Classic that was only a year old, and it was the nicest car I'd ever sat in. She drove it at two speeds: gas pedal to the floor and lurching stop. We pinballed through traffic all the way into Farmington. I had to keep my eyes on the road to keep from throwing up. Mrs. Nelson turned the heat on full blast, and I quickly regretted wearing a coat.

We reached the lawyer's office at 4:55. I jumped out and tore off my coat, relieved to be on solid ground and out of the inferno inside the Caprice. There was a sign in front of the building with large brass letters that read COLE, PARKINSON, AND PALMER. Mrs. Nelson walked right past the reception area without saying a word and began to weave through a maze of desks and chairs. Girls in skirts and dresses were getting ready to leave for the day. They looked at us curiously, but Mrs. Nelson just kept walking while I trailed with my head down. We reached a desk behind which sat a tall lady with bright red hair. She looked up and smiled very cheerfully.

"Hello, miss," began Mrs. Nelson, "is Mr. Palmer in?"

"Do you have an appointment with him?" the lady asked as she looked us over.

"Well, no, but I need to see him for a few minutes. He's been helping me with some business."

"Oh, right. You've been here before. Well, he was about to leave, and he hates to see anyone without an appointment. But since he made me take a short lunch today, I think we could impose on him a little." She let out a mischievous giggle and then whispered, "Besides, I don't think he's actually doing anything except reading a magazine."

We followed her toward a closed door. She gave a couple of short knocks and then opened it. A man in a white shirt and tie threw down the magazine he was reading and stood up.

"Some clients to see you, Mr. Palmer," said the red-haired lady.

"What? I, uh . . . It's almost five. What's this about?" he stammered, trying very hard to remember something.

"You've been helping me with my will, remember?" Mrs. Nelson cut in.

"Oh, yes, that's right. I thought we'd finished that. Have you changed your mind already?"

Mr. Palmer was still standing behind his desk when Mrs. Nelson sat down in one of the chairs on the other side of it.

"This will just take a minute. Let me introduce you to my neighbor Jackson," she said, gesturing toward me.

Mr. Palmer stuck out a soft, chubby hand, and I shook it cautiously. "Pleased to meet you," he said automatically.

I suddenly felt very underdressed and realized I was the only one wearing jeans and a T-shirt.

"Well, I guess you might as well sit down for a minute," said Mr. Palmer as he sunk back into his chair with a defeated look.

"I'll just be back at my desk," called the red-haired lady as she backed out of the office with a big smile.

"Thank you," Mr. Palmer replied sarcastically. He turned toward Mrs. Nelson and asked, "Okay, what can I do for you?"

"Jackson and I have made an agreement we want to

formalize," she began, and then she described our conversations from the past two days. Mr. Palmer's expression turned from bored to confused.

"Let me get this straight. You want to give Jackson the orchard property, so you want me to change your will? Just a week ago all of it was going to your son."

"Oh, I'm not giving Jackson the orchard. He's going to earn it. Well, that is if he can keep his part of our agreement and show he's the true heir. You know, like I explained," she responded, getting excited.

"You want me to take the orchard out of the will so you can maybe give it to Jackson?" he asked, growing frustrated.

"Well, I guess you should do that, too, but I also want you to draw up a formal agreement between Jackson and me. Like a contract that says if he does so-and-so, I do such-and-such."

The top of Mr. Palmer's bald head began to turn red. "I've got to tell you, Mrs. Nelson, this is highly unorthodox. Certainly not the kind of thing with which I am typically involved."

"It is unusual, maybe, but we already agreed. So if you would just please write something down that we could sign, we could then leave you alone."

Mr. Palmer looked like he wanted to yell at or maybe even kick someone. He looked at me, and I thought he had chosen his target. "And you want to do this? Sign your name to something and all that?" he asked, glaring at me.

"That's what we agreed to," I answered weakly, and shrugged my shoulders.

"Oh, all right! Jean, get in here," he called toward the door.

The red-haired lady walked in instantly, as if she had been standing just outside the door. She was holding a pad of paper and had a big grin on her face. Mr. Palmer began to recite some words that sounded very official in phrases like "it is agreed between the two parties." Mrs. Nelson would frequently interrupt him to correct details of the contract.

"It's $8,000 earned from apple sales, Mr. Palmer. Make sure you put in 'within a single growing season' too."

Jean was writing furiously on her paper and giggled when Mrs. Nelson would say something. Finally, Mr. Palmer looked up some numbers off a document that sounded like they described where the orchard was located.

"Now go type that up quickly, Jean, so we can get out of here. Oh, yes, what's your last name, Jackson?"

"Jones," I said, as Jean hurried out of the room to her typewriter.

Clack, clack, click, clack came the sound from outside the door. The three of us stared around the office uncomfortably. To break the tension, I said, "She's a really fast typist."

"She better be," replied Mr. Palmer, looking away from us and out the window toward the parking lot.

When Jean returned, she kept smiling and chuckling to herself. She laid the piece of paper out on the desk in front of us. The same names were on the top of the paper as those I had seen above the door while we were walking into the building. There were places for Mrs. Nelson and me to sign our names. She signed "Violet Nelson." I hadn't known what her first name was before. I admired her signature for a couple of seconds before signing mine. My signature looked like a five-year-old's next to hers. Mr. Palmer signed as a witness, and it was done.

"So all nice and legal, huh?" Mrs. Nelson asked cheerfully.

"I don't know. Maybe. As long as you think so," mumbled Mr. Palmer, who was busy putting on a coat and stuffing things into his briefcase.

"Could I have a copy of it too? For my records?" I asked timidly.

Mr. Palmer looked back at me and gave his first grin. "Yeah, Jean, make him a copy. I'm sure you wouldn't mind staying a little later to do that and then showing them out. But I've got to go." And with that, he walked out of the office.

I had heard a lot about them but had never seen a copying machine work before. We were still getting ditto handouts in all my classes. It took Jean a few minutes to warm up the thing. I watched in awe as a flash of light swept over the typed page and a piece of paper that looked like a grayer, blurrier version of the original slid out.

It was already dark when we got home. I hurried back to my house and into my room before anyone could ask questions. I took my copy of the contract, folded it in two, and put it in between the pages of the single encyclopedia volume I had on a shelf. I had gotten it when they were having a promotion at the supermarket. They pretty much gave you the first volume, hoping you'd buy the rest of them. For one penny I got A–Ar. I filed the contract under "Apple" and rushed out before anyone came looking for me.

Chapter 3
HELP! ANYONE?

I sneaked into the kitchen and joined the rest of my family for dinner. Upon seeing me, my mom instantly asked, "When did you come in? So what did you do to help Mrs. Nelson?"

"Oh, well, I think she just wanted some company."

"Really? Mrs. Nelson? A sixty-five-year-old woman wants you for company?"

"I also carried some stuff," I added quickly. In my mind "the stuff" was my copy of the contract and I had actually carried it home. So I felt that the last statement did have at least some truth to it.

"Well, that makes more sense. I guess it's nice that you're friendly with her. She's kind of kept to herself most of the time, but she's still our neighbor," Mom concluded, in what I hoped was the end of that conversation.

"'Kept to herself' is an interesting way of putting it," Dad blurted out. "Remember how she wouldn't speak to you for the first five years we were here?" He had a sarcastic grin on his face.

"Let's try not to judge Mrs. Nelson, honey," Mom said, staring at Dad with a determined look on her face. "If she's trying to be friendly to Jackson, he should be happy to be friendly back."

"That's not what you said . . ." Dad began, but was abruptly cut off when Mom gave him a scowl and motioned her head toward my sisters and me. He gave a little eye roll and shook his head.

I lay in bed that night thinking about what might be ahead of me. Now that the deal with Mrs. Nelson was "maybe" legal, I needed to figure out how to raise apples. But what made apples grow and how did you get them off the trees? Maybe you didn't have to do much. An apple tree naturally wants to make apples. I just had to let them come.

———————

Since I had mentally committed myself to the orchard, when I got to school the next day, I began telling a few friends how I was taking over the old Nelson place. No one seemed to care until I started bragging about how much money I was going to make.

"Oh, I'm sure you will 'cause there are tons of Mexicans who come up here to get rich picking fruits and vegetables," Chad Heslop said sarcastically while copying my math homework. That got things rolling, and before I knew it, variations of "Jackson Appleseed" were being invented all around me. There was no use fighting back, so I put my head on my desk, wishing I had kept my big mouth shut.

I decided that afternoon that I was going to be the greatest apple farmer there ever was just to show those idiots. I also decided I should keep the details of Mrs. Nelson's agreement to myself. There had been enough laughing without telling everyone that I might be doing it all for nothing if I wasn't the "true heir." That provision would have to remain a secret between Violet Nelson, the encyclopedia, and me.

When I got off the bus after school, instead of following my sisters and cousins down the road that led around the orchard and to our houses, I turned left and walked through the orchard itself. This had always seemed like forbidden territory before, but now I felt like I belonged. I ran my fingers up and down the reddish-brown trunk of the nearest tree, feeling the rough bark and all the knotholes. The branches looked naked and wild in their winter state, with hundreds, maybe thousands of little shoots going off in all directions.

I first walked south, counting ten trees in that direction. Then I walked east, counting trees as I went. The middle of the orchard looked much more overgrown with weeds than the outside. The little ditches next to the trees were caved in and barely recognizable. The trees seemed taller too. When I had counted to ten, I found a plow abandoned between two trees. A couple of rows farther, there was a funny-looking machine that was flat on top and looked like it was supposed to be pulled by a tractor. Instead of wheels, though, it had lots of round metal discs attached inside it that looked like they would spin around as it moved.

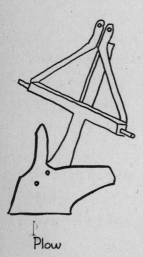

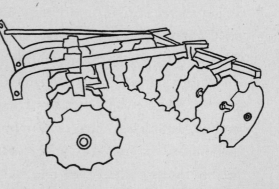

Plow

Funny machine with metal discs

By the time I counted twenty rows, I didn't feel as welcome anymore. By thirty, I felt the same way I had when I was looking at Mrs. Nelson's signature compared to mine. There were three hundred trees all right, all of them more than twice as tall as I was.

Mrs. Nelson was waving at me from the dirt road when I came out of the orchard. I was sure she had been watching me through a window the whole time. "I see you're walking through the orchard, inspecting all the trees," she said excitedly as I walked up to her.

"Uh-huh. Three hundred seems like a lot when you count them up close."

"My husband always thought that three hundred was a lucky number, at least for trees, I guess."

"Mrs. Nelson, do you know what that machine is in the orchard next to the plow?"

"No, not really."

"I've kind of been thinking that if I'm going to raise $8,000 worth of apples, maybe I should be working on the orchard already. You know, getting it ready for apple growing. What's the first thing I should do? Can you even do anything while it's still winter?"

From the look on Mrs. Nelson's face, I could tell that she had no idea what to tell me. I thought of asking her if she had actually ever been in the orchard before but stopped myself.

"Well, my husband was always doing something in there, even in the winter. He never really told me what it was, though," she replied, after what seemed a few moments of her deepest concentration. We both turned to look at the trees, until she finally said, "I'm going in. It's freezing out here. I just wanted to see how things were going so far."

"Thanks," I whispered.

I turned and started toward my house. I really wanted to ask my dad for advice. Even if he didn't know specifically about apples, he always seemed to figure out every problem that popped up around the house. Talking to him would be tricky. I had to first tell him I couldn't work at Slim's scrap yard and then convince him that trying to raise apples for Mrs. Nelson was a good idea. He would have to be in the right mood, and I would have to warm him up slowly. Just springing a new idea on him always ended badly for me. Once, I had interrupted an argument he was having with my mom about the way she ironed his shirts. I announced I was growing my hair long and feathering it like the kids on the TV show *Eight Is Enough*. We immediately left for Farmington and drove around until we found an open barber shop. Dad told the barber to give me a "going into the army" cut.

Over the next two days, I watched for the right opportunity. By Friday night I was getting desperate because I knew Dad was planning to drag me to Slim Nickle's the next day. I found myself alone with him as he tried to fix our washing machine. It was a risky environment because his mood basically depended on how the repairs were going. If the reported leak wasn't located and fixed within an hour, even if I told him Mrs. Nelson was giving me a million dollars, he would think it was a bad idea.

I prayed for the best and started in. "So how does it look?"

Dad rattled off his theories on what might be wrong and his plan of attack as I repeated "uh-huh" after every explanation.

"Dad, what did Mom mean when she said that Mrs. Nelson used to keep to herself a lot?" I asked after a couple minutes of silence.

The question caught him a little off-guard, but he grinned and seemed happy to discuss the topic. "Don't tell your mom I told you, but when we first moved in here, Violet Nelson was not happy about it at all," he said in a quiet voice, as if he were explaining a government conspiracy.

"Why not?"

"Well, the Nelsons used to own all of this property,

including our lot and your uncle's lot. Then they had some financial crisis and had to sell off a chunk. That's when we moved in and built these houses. Old Lady Nelson acted like we were really trashing up the place."

"How about Mr. Nelson? What was he like?"

"Jack Nelson? He was okay. He would stop and talk to me if he saw me, but only if he was by himself. Pretty quiet."

"What did he do for a job?"

"Oh, sold insurance or something like that. Why?"

"Just wondering why he planted that orchard in front. To make extra money?"

"I doubt it. Probably more of a hobby. Always trying to get his son to help him with it, but I think he liked sitting in the house more."

"You mean Tommy?"

"That's the one. The baby boy. Hand me that screwdriver."

"So did you ever watch Mr. Nelson in the orchard? I mean, do you know what kind of things he had to do to get the apples to grow?"

"No, not really. I never wanted to be a farmer."

My heart sank. He probably wasn't going to be much help in terms of advice.

"Ha-ha!" Dad yelled out. "I tell you what I am, a mechanical genius! It's fixed! No more leak. I'll bet that saved us fifty bucks," he said with a toothy smile on his face and arms in the air. He looked down at me and then remembered our conversation. "So why you asking about that orchard?"

This was my chance. He was never in a better mood than after having saved some money.

"Mrs. Nelson asked me to help raise some apples this year. It would be like a job."

Dad gave me a long look. "Oh yeah? How much is she going to pay you?"

"I'd get a part of everything we sell."

"Which part?"

"Depends on how many we sell, I guess, but it could be a lot of money. And I would be working after school, too, not just during the summer."

Dad let out a little "hmm," which meant he liked the idea of me sitting around as little as possible.

"And I'd be close to the house all the time, in case Mom needed me for something."

"I hate for you to miss your shot with Slim." Dad looked thoughtfully at the washer. "I guess it'll be all right," he finally drawled. "As long as this orchard thing is legit. You're not just making the whole thing up to get out of real work?"

"No! I promise. It's real. I was just going to ask you if you knew how I should get started. Mrs. Nelson is not much help."

"Oh brother. A prima donna old lady and a kid who

doesn't know the difference between an apple and his armpit. I'm sure you two will be rolling in money."

I flushed red and looked at the floor. "Well, do you know anyone I could talk to about getting started?"

"You're smart. You'll figure it out. It can't be too hard. There are plenty of people around here raising apples, and no Einsteins in the bunch." Dad started putting his tools away and mumbling about me "giving up a perfectly good job to sharecrop for some old lady." We then walked triumphantly into the kitchen together to fish for compliments from my mom for fixing the washing machine.

Even if he wasn't any help, at least Dad had accepted the idea. Maybe that was the best I could hope for. If everything worked out, he would probably be proud of the great deal I negotiated. Still, it was scary to not be able to rely on my dad for answers. I couldn't remember a time when that had ever happened. It felt like I had been driven out into the desert and abandoned.

For the entire weekend, I thought about everyone I knew and whether they might have a history with apples and, more importantly, whether they'd be willing to help. As I sat staring blankly at the bookcase in our living room, an idea finally bubbled up from somewhere in my brain. What about a book? In sixth grade I had to do a research report on a subject picked out of a hat. I got the Roman Empire and was told I had to use two books besides the encyclopedia. If there were books about something like the Roman Empire, maybe there were books with useful information, too, like how to raise apples. I checked my A–AR encyclopedia volume where I had filed the contract but didn't find nearly enough apple-growing details. I would have to try to find a whole book on the subject somewhere at the library.

———\

On Monday I noticed that none of the kids at school carried any books besides their class textbooks. In elementary school we used to have scheduled library times, and some people would constantly check out books. Percy Collyer read every Hardy Boys book there was. In junior high, though, he was bookless.

"Hey, Percy, why aren't you carrying around a book, reading all the time like you used to?" I asked him as we walked between classes.

"I dunno. Never been to the library here, I guess," he said, shrugging.

Come to think of it, neither had I. I didn't even know where the library was, or if one existed. It was time to find out. Since we didn't have any library time in our schedules, I decided I would ask to leave one of my classes early to go find it. The most likely time would be during history.

After the opening bell, I raced through the reading

and ditto handout Mr. Clafton had given us. I grabbed my textbook and made my way up to the front of the room, where Mr. Clafton was sitting casually behind his desk.

"There he is! Mr. Jones! Working hard or hardly working?" he asked with a big smile and his feet up.

"Working hard, I guess," I replied, wondering if this was a real question and whether I was supposed to answer it.

"So what's up? Is this new tie awesome or what?" he asked, lovingly stroking a shiny, very thin tie.

"Pretty cool. Mr. Clafton, I'm done with my reading and questions, so I was wondering if I could get a hall pass to go somewhere."

"Sure, if you're all done. Where do you want to go?" he asked, reaching for a stack of hall passes inside his desk.

"I was hoping to get a book from the library."

His feet fell from the desk, and his smile turned into a squinty-eyed stare. "Well, Mrs. Vance, the librarian, doesn't like kids leaving class to go there."

"When are we supposed to go, then? During lunch?"

"No, she's closed during lunch."

"Before school?"

"No, and she closes after school too. If you want something to read, why don't you go check my shelves? I've got some cool books and magazines."

"But I wanted to get something specific. Maybe something about history." I thought throwing in that last line might appeal to him as a teacher. I could see the struggle going on inside Mr. Clafton's head. His face was a mixture of fear and recklessness. After staring me down for a few seconds, he finally responded.

"Okay, but don't tell her whose class you're from."

His anxiety was contagious, and I second-guessed my plan as I took the hall pass from his hands. "So where exactly is the library?"

He explained quickly and then looked away from me. I walked through the maze of hallways that led to the secret location. It was well hidden, near the end of what I thought was an unfinished part of school.

I paused after grabbing the door handle, trying to imagine what was inside that had Mr. Clafton so spooked. I thought of turning back, but then remembered the scrap yard and pulled hard.

The door opened into a huge, brightly lit room with rows and rows of books along every wall stacked up to the ceiling. There were no posters or signs anywhere. Every book seemed to be filed on a shelf. In the middle of the room, a woman with large, gray and black hair looked up from a book. She narrowed her eyes over her small glasses and demanded, "What do you want?"

I walked toward her and said feebly, "I have a hall pass."

"From whom?" she almost shouted.

"Umm, from my history teacher. Could you help me find a book on apples or apple farming?"

"What? Of course not! Don't you know what a card catalog is for?" She glanced over at a wooden box with lots of wooden drawers, and I quickly moved toward it.

With nervous fingers, I thumbed my way through the drawer that started with AP until I reached a section that seemed to have books about apples. Out jumped a card for the perfect book: *The Growth and Care of Apple Trees,* by Jeffrey Haslam. Nonfiction, 348 pages, illustrated, 634 H64.

What did those numbers mean? I knew they must somehow tell me where the book was. I looked up at Mrs. Vance. She had one eye on me, her expression cold. I memorized the number and moved over to the nearest stack of books. I had fifteen minutes until the class period was over. My eyes darted back and forth. I realized I might never get another chance at this. The numbers on the sides of the books were all in the 400s. I changed rows, moving toward the far wall, and realized the numbers were getting smaller. I moved in the other direction, skipping a few rows. The whole time I felt Mrs. Vance's icy stare. I ended up in a 600 row and scanned down the shelves until I saw 634. I moved my fingers over the books until I had the exact call number and pulled the book from the shelf. It looked like it had never been opened. I thumbed through it, looking at some of the pictures. There were diagrams and charts, even illustrations on how to do things. I couldn't believe my luck!

Clutching the book to my chest, sweat pouring down my back, I walked toward the desk in front of Mrs. Vance. The clock behind her said there were five minutes left in the class period.

"I would like to check out this book, please . . . ma'am," I squeaked, holding the book out in front of me. She snatched it from my hands and inspected it carefully. She looked up at me, thinking of a reason to say no. Finally, she opened a drawer and pulled out a set of cards. She selected one and wiped off the dust.

"Name?" she barked.

"Jackson Jones . . . ma'am."

She wrote my name on the card, pulled out another card in the little envelope inside the front cover of the book, and wrote my name on that one too. She stuck the first card back in the book and held it up. Then she yanked it away before I could grab it and growled, "Have it back here in two weeks."

"I will," I said as she finally let go of the book. I turned and walked quickly toward the exit, not wanting to look back in case she changed her mind. I threw the doors wide open just as the bell rang for the next period.

Cool relief filled my whole body. Looking down at the book, I exhaled loudly through my mouth, as if I'd been holding my breath for the last fifteen minutes. I held the book high over my head like a trophy and walked victoriously to my locker.

Chapter 4
NO ONE WORKS FOR FREE

The afternoon after my library visit, I ran all the way home from the bus stop and shut myself in my room. I cracked open the apple book and only stopped reading grudgingly to eat dinner. I did a lot of skimming so I could get through it quickly. As I got closer to the end, panic gripped me. There was much more to raising apples than I had thought. The book explained a lot, but I could only keep it for two weeks. I needed that copier I saw in Mr. Palmer's office but decided I would do the only thing available to me. I grabbed a spiral notebook and started hand copying important sections.

At first I copied whole paragraphs word for word, but then moved on to writing down titles and important sentences. I woke up the next morning with my face pressed on top of the book and my written pages scattered all over the floor. By the next night, I forced myself to stop copying. There was so much to actually do that I didn't think I should spend any more time just reading about it. I tried to organize all the necessary work into categories and even drew out a calendar of what needed to be done and when. It was a mess of chicken-scratch writing and crooked lines, but phenomenal compared to what I would usually turn in for homework.

According to the book, the first thing you needed to do was prune, and you were supposed to start during the winter. It involved cutting off part of the branches on a tree. This didn't make a lot of sense, but by then I completely trusted Mr. Jeffrey Haslam and everything he had written about apples. My calendar allowed for six weeks of pruning starting right then.

Three hundred trees in six weeks would mean fifty trees every week. I could probably only work three hours after school before it started to get dark and then maybe twelve hours on Saturday. There was no way my mom would let me work on Sunday, since it was against the Ten Commandments, so I knew that day was completely out. That meant twenty-seven hours per week or about two trees an hour! Thinking back on how big and wild the trees looked, and how many branches I'd have to remove, I knew it would be impossible for one person. And there were a ton of things to do after pruning too! Maybe my friends were right to laugh at me without even knowing why. At some point during the summer, my dad would figure out how hopeless it all was and drag me down to be Slim's slave.

TREES TO PRUNE EACH WEEK

300 Total trees
÷ 6 Weeks
_____

50 Trees per week

HOURS PER WEEK FOR PRUNING

3 Hours per day (Mon–Fri)
x 5 Days per week (Mon–Fri)
_____

15 Hours (Mon–Fri)
+ 12 Hours on Saturday
_____

27 Hours per week

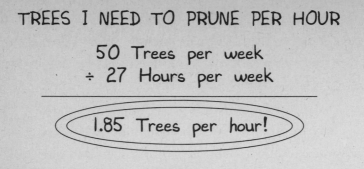

TREES I NEED TO PRUNE PER HOUR

50 Trees per week
÷ 27 Hours per week

1.85 Trees per hour!

The next afternoon I saw Mrs. Nelson waving at me from her house. A feeling of humiliation oozed through me. Was she just making fun of me too? She must know all this was impossible. I decided to go talk to her and find out exactly what she was thinking.

"Come in, come in, Jackson," she said happily as she opened the door.

"Hi," I said as I walked in, not bothering to wipe my feet very carefully. I sat in the nearest chair and launched into my first question. "Mrs. Nelson, when your husband was running the orchard, did he have another job too?"

"Oh, of course."

"So how many hours a week would he spend working out there?"

"Well, that was always different for different times of the year. At the busiest, he would be out there every night after work and on the weekends."

"And he did all the work by himself?" I asked with a hint of sarcasm.

"He always wanted Tommy to be out there with him, but"—she paused for a moment—"that didn't always work out. Some days I think he would go hire people to help him."

"Hire people? What people?"

"Oh, I don't know. Just people looking for some temporary work."

I imagined Mr. Nelson bringing home twenty people to boss around in the orchard. If he wasn't doing the work, no wonder he thought it was so wonderful.

"So how am I supposed to run the whole thing by myself when he had help? I'm just a kid!" I blurted out with some resentment in my voice. I watched her face. I was waiting for it to break into laughter, proving that this was all just a little joke. Her expression didn't change, however. She just sat there looking concerned but hopeful.

"I guess I never really considered all of that. There's nothing to stop you from getting some help too."

"How am I supposed to hire anyone? I don't have any money to pay them. I wouldn't even know where to find anyone."

She just smiled at me and said, "I'm sure you'll find a way." Then she patted my shoulder. I had heard expressions like that from adults many times before. When my mom or dad said them, it made me think that in the end they would always be there to fix the problem if they had to. With Mrs. Nelson, the words seemed empty, just sounds coming from a mouth. I wondered again whether she had ever been in that orchard before.

"Oh, I almost forgot," she continued. "I showed our contract to Tommy today. You should have seen his face. It was priceless. Didn't think I'd do it, huh?" She chuckled to herself smugly.

"I hope he doesn't get mad at me," I said, wondering if she'd explained it was her idea.

"Don't you worry about Tommy. I told him how happy I am to have you out in that orchard. You just need to concentrate on apples."

I was tempted at that point to forget the whole thing. It was pretty easy to see she was using me to make some kind of point with her son and expecting me to do the work of a whole team of people. The only thing that kept me going was the thought of explaining the situation to my dad. He'd probably sign me to a lifetime contract with Slim.

If things had any hope of working out, I needed to find some cheap labor fast. Specifically, I needed employees who didn't require me to pay them, at least not immediately, and were available whenever I needed them. They would also need to be understanding, or at least not vengeful, if the operation fell apart in the end. Oh, and used to being in the cold. I decided this was the type of employee I had to be related to.

Between my immediate family and my uncle's family, there were plenty of relatives to choose from. My dad and uncle were brothers and had built houses next to each other before I was even old enough to remember. I had mentally crossed off my dad and uncle from the list of potential employees. They both were always complaining about how tired they were and how much they had to do around the house already. I was never sure why they were so tired or what they did all day. My dad worked at some place that sold bolts. He almost never talked about his job at home, but when he did it was about missing bolt orders, "worthless salesmen," and "Old Man Scott," who I think was his boss. Uncle David worked at the power plant like a lot of other men where we lived. It was hard to say exactly what he did there, but the place used a lot of coal and produced electricity, so it had to be something to do with one of those things.

My mom didn't have a job, but she made it clear that she was always worn out by the time she put her kids to bed. To tell the truth, I never really knew what she did during the day either. Mom did like working outside, however, and would plant flowers every spring that wouldn't survive the summer. I considered her a faint possibility for the orchard. My aunt Sandy was kind of like a second mom, only funnier. Of the four adults, I would probably have confided in her first about Mrs.

Nelson's contract. I knew she would have thought it was funny and not just the kind of funny where she was laughing at me. I couldn't see asking her for help with the work, though.

My only real hope rested with my two younger sisters and three cousins. Common sense said to find someone with a little farming experience, but I actually liked the fact that they would know even less about raising apples than I did. If I was going to be making a lot of mistakes and bad decisions, at least they wouldn't know any better. Besides, if this was going to be my orchard, I didn't want anyone else acting like they ran the place.

Talking them into helping wasn't going to be easy. My sisters had stopped listening to me years before, and my cousins were usually devoted to watching whatever was on TV. It was critical for me to first convince my cousin Amy, who was the oldest of the group. My sisters wanted to be like her and her two younger brothers respected her. She was much more persuasive than I was. All in all, I'd feel more confident with her around.

Amy was only four months older than me but a grade ahead. Growing up, we mostly had each other to play with since anyone else our age lived too far away. Most games involved her telling me what to do while I tried to control our little brothers and sisters. At school Amy constantly watched out for me, which meant something because she was way more popular than I could ever hope to be. With every passing year, the age gap between us seemed to grow. Unfortunately, she had stopped wanting to be outside much and almost seemed embarrassed sometimes that she lived down a dirt road. I knew I couldn't call what we had to do in the orchard "farming" because she would immediately refuse. I would try explaining how much money we would make—she was always complaining about not having any. Maybe I'd even beg. I was willing to try anything, really.

The day after my latest visit with Mrs. Nelson, I followed Amy home from school and told her I had to ask her something in private. She smiled, looked around, and said, "Okay, let's go to my room," as if we were about to swap secret passwords. I knew she thought it was either about a girl I liked or, better yet, about a boy she liked.

Her room was newly decorated with Michael Jackson posters. Once inside, she stopped in front of her mirror to comb and admire her hair. She used to wear it in ponytails but had cut it short at the beginning of the school year, right about the time she started watching MTV. We didn't get it where we lived, but Amy had some friends in Farmington and she would stay over at their houses for all-night MTV marathons.

"Okay, so what did you want to tell me?" she asked excitedly once she was satisfied with her hair.

I didn't want to seem like I didn't have any interesting information and I wanted to make sure she was in a positive state of mind, so I said, "Someone asked me about you and wants to know if you're going with anyone or not."

"Really? Who was it?"

"I promised I wouldn't tell you that he told me."

"Bobby? Jason? Umm . . . Troy?" she asked, starting to giggle.

"I can't say, but I think you might already like him."

I was amazed at how readily she believed me. I guess it was because she wanted to. A blush came across her cheeks. She explained to me exactly what I was supposed to say back to the person and what I was supposed to look for in his facial expressions when I told him.

After thirty minutes she was still giggling and had moved to sitting on her bed while I sat cross-legged on the floor. I decided it was time. I'd start by talking about money.

"So do you remember that one summer when we saw that show about shipwrecks and then dug up our yards looking for gold?"

"Yeah, sure. Why?" she asked with a suspicious look coming over her face.

"I don't know. I just thought it was funny because it would be nice to have money like that for clothes or even a car someday."

"Paige Manning's dad says he's going to buy her a car when she turns sixteen. Probably a new one. I bet I have to get rides to school when I'm sixteen."

"So would you rather be rich and have the nicest car in the world, or be the cutest girl in school?"

"Definitely the cutest, because you can always get a job for things like a car."

"So where would you work, then?"

"I don't know. It's like you need a car first to drive anywhere."

"I know, I know," I said, acting like I was deep in thought. I looked up at her and stared into her eyes.

"What are you staring at?" she asked nervously.

"That summer we were doing all the digging was when you broke your mom's music box. Remember how I took the blame because you said she wouldn't be able to punish me as much."

"Yeah, yeah. So what does that have to do with anything?"

"You promised that you'd owe me some huge favor in the future if I kept quiet and let her be mad at me."

"I did? Are you sure?" She laughed nervously, afraid of the answer.

"Definitely sure. And I need that favor now. But it's also a way to earn money without a car."

"I'm not sure a promise like that counts when you're only nine or however old we were."

"Oh, it counts. It definitely counts."

She looked at me anxiously.

"It's not like I'm going to ask you to do something illegal—I just need your help. And you'd get paid," I said, trying hard to reassure her.

"So what is it?" she asked after a few awkward seconds.

"Mrs. Nelson wants me to get her apple orchard growing again and sell the apples. But I can't do it all myself. I need you to help me and then you can have part of the money we earn."

"What? Why would you want to do that? You don't know anything about growing apples. It sounds crazy!"

"I know. I know. But I'm figuring it out. We really just have to get the apples to grow, pick 'em, and sell 'em."

"But why would you want to do it in the first place?"

"It's either that or work at the scrap yard with Skeeter Nickles."

"Oh." A slight look of sympathy crossed over her face. "So when are you planning for all this to happen? In the summer or something?"

"In the summer, yeah, and there are also things we need to start doing now."

"It doesn't sound very fun. Why are you asking me, anyway?"

"Because I like you. And you're the toughest, hardest-working person I know."

"Yeah right. You couldn't think of anyone else, could you?" she said with a smirk.

I looked into her face again. I wanted to tell her everything about Mrs. Nelson's agreement and about the fact that I had no idea what I was doing. I wanted to confess that I was scared I was going to fail and waste everyone's time, but that if she would do this with me, I had a tiny bit of hope it was possible. I looked at the floor and was only able to manage, "Amy, this is something I really want to do, and I know I can't do it without you. If you help me, I will never forget it and always owe you."

She didn't reply at first but lay back on her bed, looking at the ceiling and playing with her hair. The seconds ticked by. "Oh, all right!" she said in a voice of surrender. "But we're going to make lots of money, right?"

"It'll be like growing money on trees," I replied excitedly, repeating Mrs. Nelson's line. "But we'll have to work hard."

"I'm only working as hard as you do."

"Will you really?"

"No, not really, but I could promise you if you like," she said sarcastically. "And this doesn't seem like a very fair trade of favors. All you had to do was act like you broke that stupid music box."

"Are you kidding? Your mom reminds me of it every

time I'm in your living room. That's gonna last my whole life. All I'm asking from you is one crop of apples."

Amy sat up and rolled her eyes.

"You know, we could probably use my sisters and your brothers if they would do it," I added.

"Are they going to get part of the huge fortune too?"

"I guess they would have to, but there should be plenty to go around."

"Like how much?"

"Thousands probably."

"Thousands? Hmm. Well, if you can convince them to actually work, it might be all right."

"I'll go talk to everyone. Maybe I'll tell them that the amount they would get depends on how much work I think they could do."

"Yeah, I guess."

"Okay, so we'll start tomorrow?" I asked enthusiastically. "I need you to come with me to Mrs. Nelson's to get some stuff."

"Tomorrow? I can't believe I said I'd do it." She sighed as she dropped back onto her bed.

I was mostly happy that Amy had agreed to help, but I felt a little guilty about our conversation. First, no boy had really asked me about her, although this seemed like just a small stretch of the truth. I was sure that there were *plenty* of boys at school who liked her and would like to know more about her. I felt worse telling her about getting money after we sold all the apples. It was kind of true, though, because we would get everything over $8,000, plus the orchard itself had to be worth money. I'd be happy to split that with her if she wanted. Somehow the money details would just have to be worked out later. That was so far into the future, it seemed unreal. For now, we just needed to get things started.

After talking with Amy, I spoke with each of the younger kids that night, starting with my cousin Sam. He was eleven and was like a very energetic puppy constantly moving and searching for something. The instant I mentioned that Amy and I were going to be working together, he wanted to be a part of it. At first he suggested having his own set of trees to take care of and even volunteered to take half of the orchard. It took ten minutes to convince him that probably wasn't a good idea. He wanted to start that night, even though it was almost completely dark outside. I started talking about what part of the earnings he could make before I realized that he was more than willing to work for nothing. In the end we agreed that he should have 11 percent since he was eleven. That reasoning really appealed to Sam.

My cousin Michael was a more difficult case. He was nine and the only true loner in our family. Sometimes

I wouldn't see him for days at a time. He also wasn't very good at following instructions, but I was a desperate employer and willing to sign up anyone. During our conversation, I eventually had to resort to stroking his ego by telling him that Amy and I didn't think we could do it without him. He was very interested in the money and how much of it he could make and kept repeating, "Well, I don't think you can do it without me." He started by demanding half of any money but had to accept the logic that if Sam was older and getting 11 percent, he should be happy with less. We settled on 9 percent since, of course, he was nine. I also told him that his percentage would go down if he didn't work hard. He repeated, "You won't be able to do it without me."

My sisters were hard to convince too. Lisa was ten and didn't seem all that interested in the money, but was concerned she might be left out of something everyone else was doing. She also didn't like the idea of working after school because she might get bad grades if she couldn't do her homework.

"I want to go to college, you know, and you have to get good grades all the way down to kindergarten," she said matter-of-factly.

"How is a college supposed to know what your grades were in elementary school?"

"They check. They call the school and find out. Our teacher told us so."

I couldn't argue with her. Our years together had taught me that much. In the end we agreed that she would work only on Saturdays, but she had to do it without complaining or she couldn't be part of the team. Dividing the money by age seemed to make a lot of sense now, so we agreed on 10 percent for her.

My youngest sister, Jennifer, was eight. She wanted to do just what Lisa did, so she was only available on Saturdays too. She also didn't want to work near her boy cousins. I thought she would only be good for about 3 percent, but I figured it was best to stay with the age system, so she got 8.

By the end of that night, I had given away a large chunk of future apple money. It may have been more than 100 percent, but I was too afraid to add it up. I had the same bad feelings I had had after talking with Amy. I knew I could make it right, though, even if I had to give everyone a part of the orchard once Mrs. Nelson handed it over. They might all quit after the first day, anyway. Except for Sam. I had a feeling that those trees would be seeing a lot of him in the future whether they liked it or not.

Chapter 5
FROSTBITE AND HARD FALLS

When we got home from school the next day, I quickly went into my house to look for my mom's clippers. She used them when she gardened, and I thought they might be helpful for the pruning that lay ahead. I finally found them in my dad's toolbox and ran out of the house. I did, however, slow down long enough to grab the apple book and give my two sisters dirty looks on the way out for not being willing to help on school days. They were sitting at the kitchen table doing their homework and pretending not to notice me.

I went over to my cousins' house and knocked on the door. "We're coming," Amy said dully, opening the door with Sam and Michael right behind her. She had changed her clothes to several layers of the shabbiest things she owned, with the top layer being a New Mexico Lobos sweatshirt her dad had gotten at a flea market.

"So what exactly are we doing?" she asked as we all started walking toward the orchard.

"I need you to come with me first. Sam and Michael, you take this book and these clippers and go wait for us by the trees closest to the road."

I led Amy toward Mrs. Nelson's house while Sam and Michael worked their way through the orchard. As I knocked on Mrs. Nelson's door, Amy whispered, "What are we doing here?"

Before I could answer, Mrs. Nelson opened the door. "Hi, Jackson! How are you?" she greeted me happily. "How are those trees?"

"Hi, Mrs. Nelson. This is my cousin Amy, and we're just coming over to talk about that."

Mrs. Nelson gave Amy a little nod.

"We're going to get started with some pruning. Do you remember your husband doing that?"

"Well, maybe," she said very thoughtfully.

"Did he have any special tools he used for it?"

"If he did, they would be in the shed behind the house."

"Do you think we could have a look and maybe use some of the things in there?"

"I don't see why not. They're just sitting in there."

The three of us walked behind Mrs. Nelson's house and opened the doors to a little building. The inside was dark and it took a few seconds for our eyes to adjust. Dust and spider webs were everywhere. There were shelves against the wall piled high with unfamiliar items, like canvas bags, metal pipes, and tangles of hoses.

"Is there anything in here that could be used for cutting branches?" I asked, almost speaking to myself.

"How about this?" Mrs. Nelson asked after pulling a tool off one of the shelves. It had two long wooden handles with curved metal blades at the point. I recognized them from the apple book.

"I think those are just what we're looking for," I said as I took them from Mrs. Nelson. I moved the wooden handles back and forth and watched the metal blades move like scissors.

"Here's another one just like it," Amy said from the corner. We searched for another ten minutes without finding more pruning tools, but we did pull two long ladders off the shelves. I thanked Mrs. Nelson, and then Amy and I started dragging the ladders and tools toward the orchard. Each ladder was heavier than I realized at

Long-handled pruning scissors
(also called shears)

first, and I was a little surprised that Amy was able to drag hers all by herself. She didn't say a word about Mrs. Nelson.

We found Sam and Michael and dropped our ladders at the very corner of the orchard. Sam had climbed to the top of a tree while Michael was throwing dirt clods at its trunk. The apple book was lying in some mud along with my mom's clippers.

I picked up the book and looked at everyone. "Okay, according to this, if we want a good crop of apples, we have to cut off some of the branches before the leaves and apples start growing on them."

"That sounds stupid. If we cut off the branches, won't there be less places for apples to grow?" Michael asked confrontationally.

"Yeah, but the book says the ones that do grow will be bigger. The trees will spend more energy growing apples and less time feeding all the branches or something."

I turned to the pages in the book on pruning that illustrated the kind of spacing between branches that was just right. Amy, Michael, and I began debating how many branches to take off the first tree and where to start cutting. We each tried the pruning scissors and found that with just a little force they could cut off branches as thick as our fingers. We were deep in discussion about how to reach the highest branches when we heard a sawing noise. Sam had run home and gotten the saw his dad usually only used for cutting down Christmas trees. Before we could stop him, a huge branch just a few feet off the ground was cut through and fell with a *thunk*.

"I'm not sure that's really the idea, Sam. We probably want to leave most of the big branches," I said, gaping at the branch on the ground.

"Yeah, okay. But at least we know this saw works pretty well," he replied with enthusiasm.

It was decided that Sam would climb each tree and

cut the thicker branches near the trunk using his saw. Amy and I would use the ladders and pruning scissors and attack the outer branches. Michael was given the clippers and told to work on the smaller branches near the ground or those he could reach standing on the first few steps of our ladders. He of course wanted one of the larger pruning tools, but after putting it to a vote, he had to settle for the clippers.

We swarmed the first tree. I made my first few cuts nervously. Every few minutes Amy and I would call to each other, "How does that look?" or, "Does this look right?" We climbed up and down the ladders consulting the book's illustrations.

Sam and Michael never questioned their own work. From the middle of the tree and over our heads, large branches were continually dropping under Sam's saw. I was beginning to worry if there would be anything left to the tree if he kept it up. The bottom branches were also suffering, although the clippers really limited the size of branches Michael could destroy.

After what seemed like an hour, Amy and I had worked our way around the outside of the tree moving our ladders four or five times. I was just about to say, "Okay, let's all get down and have a look," when there was a crashing of branches to my left followed by a thud.

Sam had fallen out of the tree and lay face-down on the cold dirt. The rest of us stared at him, stunned. He got to his feet slowly, panting, and said, "Well, the middle's all done."

We stood back and examined the tree while looking at the book for comparison.

"It looks terrible!" Michael blurted out. "And it's freezing."

"Who asked you?" said Amy turning on him angrily. "Look, it's supposed to look bad when it's just bare branches. And you two boys have to stop cutting off so much. It's almost like the whole middle and bottom are gone."

BEFORE

I agreed with her but was glad that she was the one saying it.

"Now, let's try again on the next one and be more careful," she demanded.

As she spoke, I noticed that I could see her breath because it was so cold. I also realized that my ears were freezing. I looked down at my hands, and they were bright red. I really wanted to stick them in my pockets but instead grabbed my ladder and moved it to the next tree. Out of the four of us, Amy was the only one wearing a hat and gloves. We kept working for probably

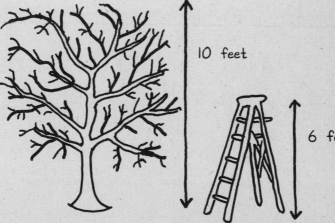

10 feet

6 feet

AFTER

another half hour. Although we seemed to be getting faster, it was also becoming much colder and darker. No one said anything, except for Michael, who complained under his breath about frostbite and losing his fingers and toes.

Amy finally said, "Why don't we go in, because I can't see anything."

I wanted to throw down the pruning scissors and run for the house, but I said, as calmly as I could, "Amy's right. Good work, guys! Let's just leave the ladders here and take the tools with us."

We walked quietly home, the boys blowing on their hands. I said goodbye as we reached my house. I left my pair of pruning scissors outside by the front door and then went in and headed straight for the heater. It took half an hour before I felt like none of my body parts were going to fall off.

"You cold out there?" Mom asked as we sat around the table.

"Not really. The work keeps you warm," I replied as cheerily as I could, looking at both of my sisters.

After dinner I went to my room and drew a map of the orchard on a piece of paper with all three hundred trees. I put an X through the tree in the farthest corner we had finished. Given how long it had taken us to prune one tree, we were going to have to get a lot faster to finish by spring. I wasn't exactly sure when that was

← To Shiprock   U.S. Highway 550   To Farmington →

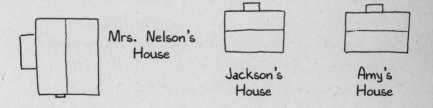

The Orchard

Dirt Road

Mrs. Nelson's House

Jackson's House

Amy's House

Desolate Land

from an apple tree's perspective, but I figured we better be done by the end of March. It was already the middle of February.

———————¬

The next day after school, I put on a knit hat, an extra coat, and the warmest gloves I could find. I grabbed my pruning tool from beside the front door and headed toward my cousins' house. Before I could knock, Amy came out leading Sam and Michael, who were dressed in as many layers as I was.

We picked up where we left off, and I noticed the apple book had been left on the ground overnight. I cringed, imagining what the librarian would say if she knew. There was a steady sound of *click, click* and the buzzing of Sam's saw against the tree. I kept saying encouraging things like "This really looks like the pictures in the book" and "I think we're moving a lot faster than yesterday." I also thought it was a good idea to keep everyone's minds off the cold by talking about shows like *The A-Team.* This made Sam and Michael wish they were watching TV while Amy ignored me completely. She kept snipping away at branches, but her face looked bored and almost angry. My mind kept imagining her throwing down the pruning scissors and just walking wordlessly away. I frantically tried to think of something to say that would keep her there.

"You know what this reminds me of?" I said. "That

time last year when Bobby Cluff was running for student council and we were hanging up signs."

"What?" Amy called back sharply.

"You know, when you were his campaign manager and I helped you hang up signs in the middle of the night so the whole school would be surprised the next day."

"Yeah, I know. I was there. But why would that remind you of anything?"

"It's just that my fingers were really cold then, too, and it got pretty dark. And there was a lot of reaching up to try and hang the signs so no one could pull them down. You know, kind of like reaching up for these branches."

Amy gave me a dismissive look that let me know she could see right through my weak attempt at psychology. She shook her head silently for a minute and then said, "I think we need a radio out here. Michael, go get the radio that Dad keeps in the washroom."

Michael trudged off and returned with the radio and began flipping through the stations. Michael Jackson's "Billie Jean" came on.

"Oh, I love this song! Leave it right there!" Amy yelled. We didn't dare argue, and she began to sing along softly to most of the songs on the station.

Counting the tree we had started on the night before, we finished three trees that Friday—and I really did think we were getting better with each one. As we were walking back home in the twilight, I asked very timidly, "So when do you want to get started tomorrow?"

"When is all this pruning supposed to be finished?" Amy asked in a frustrated voice.

"The end of March, I figure," I replied weakly.

"Oh man," she moaned, and paused while thinking. "Probably should start by eight, then," she said bitterly.

Michael whimpered, but Sam said, "I'd much rather do this than go to school."

"Great! And I'll have my sisters out here, too, so we can go really fast," I said as we separated.

I told Lisa and Jennifer about the eight o'clock start time. Before Lisa could speak, I added, "No complaining, remember?" Her mouth closed and she nodded reluctantly.

———

The next morning was very bright, and the orchard looked different than it did in the evenings. It seemed more alive. We all got to the ladders right around eight. Michael said sarcastically to my sisters, "Nice of you to join us." We decided that it would be best for them to haul the cut branches that were scattered below the finished trees into big piles in the middle of the rows. What we would do with the piles we would worry about later. For now we just had to get them out from underneath the trees. We could barely walk around because of the tangle of branches at our feet.

The two girls began dragging and pulling and forming huge spindly masses while the rest of us continued pruning. By ten it began to get so warm that I removed my top layer of coats and was beginning to feel thirsty.

"Jennifer, can you go get us some water from the house?" I called out to her.

"Why do I have to do it?" she yelled back.

"Because you're the only one we can trust."

She came back with a half-gallon pitcher and some cups. We drank quickly and didn't stop again until lunch. We all went home to eat something and then returned to the trees, the whole time eyeing one another, wondering who would quit first.

Soon I removed everything but my long-sleeved shirt, although it couldn't have been more than fifty degrees. My mom showed up with more water in the afternoon. She looked down the row of trees we had finished.

"Wow! Did you really do all of this?" she asked, staring in amazement.

At that moment Sam fell out of the tree he was working in and landed hard on the dirt. He got up without a word and took a cup of water.

"Well, it was mostly Sam," I said, turning to my mom and smiling.

We continued on until dinner. Cutting and moving the ladders, cutting and moving the ladders. By four we were too tired to talk, and the batteries in the radio had died. Michael was sent to collect every extension cord in both our houses, and he ran them from a wall plug outside my front door. For the rest of the year, we would be discovering things he had unplugged to provide those extension cords.

That Saturday we pruned twenty-two trees. We had almost three of the ten rows finished. In the middle of the rows were six huge piles of apple tree branches that Lisa and Jennifer had stacked up. As we walked home, I felt so proud of everyone that I wanted to hug them. I think they felt the same way, but no one said anything. We just kept looking back at the three rows that now looked so different from the rest.

When I said, "Thanks, everyone," before the two families separated, Michael replied, "Why are you thanking us? It's our money too."

Inside the house I took a good look at Lisa and Jennifer for the first time since that morning. Their hands and arms were covered in scratches and scrapes from the sharp branch ends. Even their faces and necks had scratches.

"Oh, Lisa, why didn't you say you were getting all scratched up like that?" I asked in a voice filled with guilt. "I could have given you my gloves."

"No complaining, remember?" she said in a defiant voice.

At that moment I regretted all the mean things I had

ever said about the two of them. I avoided their eyes and went to find some lotion to help with the scratches. I tried to help rub it on Lisa's arms, but she pulled away and grabbed the bottle.

——————→

On Sunday morning I woke with my whole body aching. I felt glad to be restricted from working for a day and only wished I could stay in bed, but Mom forced everyone to get ready for church. My sisters and I moved very slowly as we got into our church clothes and dragged through the house.

Dad thought me being in pain was great. "About time you all did some real work," he crowed. "When I was your age, I hardly had the strength left to crawl into bed after working all day."

I saw Amy at church and asked, "Are you sore?"

"What do you think, genius?" she replied.

I was nervous about what would happen on Monday and whether everyone would quit. The project seemed to have gained its own momentum, though, and my cousins showed up despite their complaints. We continued with the same system, still unsure of whether we were doing anything right. And because I had to return the library book, we didn't even have pictures to compare our work to.

Sam was the only one who wasn't moving gingerly, and Amy and I would often stop to lean one arm against our ladders just to rest our muscles a little. Whether we had pruned them correctly or not, twenty more trees were done by Friday, and there was a tangled mess of branches waiting for my sisters to pick up the next day.

Friday night I took a dollar I had been saving and asked my mom to buy a six-pack of pop in town when she went Saturday morning. The next day when we stopped for our afternoon water break, I said to everyone, "Wait here! I'll be right back."

I returned with the six-pack of grape Shasta Mom had put in the refrigerator. Everyone agreed that it was the best thing we had ever tasted. We sat in the dirt and wished we had more. Sitting there, I noticed that I could smell the cut apple branches. They were sweet, like freshly mowed grass. The dirt below us also had a smell different from the dirt on the road or in our yard. Maybe I was imagining things, but I thought it smelled a little like flowers or rain.

———\

The next week was my birthday. I was going to ask for a boom box with a cassette player—but instead asked for cases of pop. When I opened three cases of Shasta, there was a big grin on my dad's face, and I couldn't help feel that I wasn't getting the equivalent value of a boom box. Those Shastas became the high point of our Saturdays, though.

Every week we got a little faster, or maybe just more careless. The march out to the orchard after school and on Saturdays became a ritual. Sometimes I would even forget what we were doing and why we were doing it. Moving the pruning handles became as automatic as pedaling a bike. We went over the same conversation topics too—the TV show *Diff'rent Strokes,* cars, the new Farmington Mall, and Shasta flavors. By the middle of March, we were up to finishing fifty trees a week. The last week in March we did sixty. It helped that the days had gotten longer and the temperature had warmed up. Sam had also learned to hang on better in the trees.

Mrs. Nelson caught me several times on the way out to or coming back from the orchard, and she loved to talk about my "little gang of workers," as she called them. She kept telling me how beautiful the spring blossoming would be.

————————¬

One afternoon in late March, Tommy showed up in the orchard. He wandered out to where we were pruning, clumsily dodging the branches lying on the ground. I reluctantly climbed off my ladder to greet him. I wasn't sure what to say or if I should call him Tommy or Mr. Nelson. I studied his face for signs of anger or resentment. He mostly looked uncomfortable and was dressed in slacks and brown leather shoes. His body was soft and bulging in all the wrong places. He stopped about ten feet from me and pretended to be interested in one of the pruned trees.

"Hi," I called out in the friendliest voice I could muster.

"Hey. Thought I'd come check out the big reclamation project. My mom says you're going to be the new apple baron around here," Tommy replied dryly.

I couldn't tell if he was taunting me. "Yeah, she really wants to see some apples out here," I said a little defensively.

"I've been hearing that for years."

"I'm sorry to hear your mom has cancer," I said, trying to sound sincere and thoughtful.

"Shoot. She's had cancer so many times I've lost count. Any little pain she gets, she's always blaming it on cancer. I wish she'd at least think up some new disease to blame."

Tommy stared at one of the piles of branches in the middle of a row. He gave an admiring whistle. "So how many trees go into each pile?" he asked.

"Oh, about three or four," I answered proudly.

He said it reminded him of the pile of wood he had seen at a bonfire. "Be pretty amazing if you lit all of 'em up at once."

I agreed with a little laugh, and then he waved goodbye and strolled off. All and all, it was a strange conversation. Instead of being mad about what was going on in the orchard, he didn't even seem to care.

———→

We finished the last tree on March's final Saturday as the sky changed from blue into a pale pink sunset. I told everyone to wait while I ran back to my room to get my map of the orchard. We crossed off the few remaining trees and gave a little cheer.

"We're right on schedule. Can you believe it?" I asked giddily.

"So do we get paid now?" asked Michael.

Sometimes I couldn't tell whether he was serious.

"No, but I'm pretty sure the hardest part is over." Five pairs of eyes looked at me hopefully.

Chapter 6
LEARNING TO DRIVE

The relief of finishing the pruning was short-lived. After church on Sunday, all six of us went outside to the orchard to think about how to get rid of all the branches piled next to the trees. We had to assure my mom that we wouldn't be working, only thinking.

The orchard formed most of the view from the front door of my house. Out the back door was what my dad called "desolate land." It had some tumbleweeds, sagebrush, and wild grasses, but mostly it was rocks and dirt. If I went walking out there, my socks would always come back full of stickers and my mom would make me sit outside and pull them out before I was allowed into the house. The desolate land must have been owned by Mr. Nelson, because when he was alive he would pile branches in random places on it. I had never realized where he was getting the branches until we started pruning.

"Let's just take the branches out there and leave them with the older ones. I wouldn't even ask Mrs. Nelson either," Amy said forcefully as we walked through the orchard inspecting piles.

Amy seemed so determined to avoid a conversation with Mrs. Nelson that I was afraid to question her. "Yeah, she probably isn't going to care, anyway," I said, "as long as we don't drag them through her yard."

"Drag them? I'm tired of dragging them!" Lisa yelled. "Plus, it's probably half a mile from here to where we could leave them. Dragging them could take the rest of the year!"

"That's not even close to half a mile," Sam said thoughtfully.

"More like a whole mile," said Michael.

We ended up walking off the distance to end the argument. The closest possible drop zone turned out to be about a hundred yards away.

Dragging a few branches at a time did seem like a very bad idea. I told everyone that we had no choice but to turn to our "secret weapon." I knew that we would have to use it at some point, I just didn't realize it would be that soon.

Parked between my house and my cousins' house was a 1946 Ford tractor. Our families had never used it for anything agricultural. Mostly it was driven once or twice a year on what Uncle David called "hayrides." Everyone was forced to ride on a flat, rickety wagon attached to the tractor while it was pulled along the highway. No actual hay was involved. These trips usually took place around Christmas so we could look at and judge our neighbors' Christmas lights. Hayrides also took place around the Fourth of July, which seemed to be the only other time my dad or uncle remembered the tractor. Amy hated those rides and would duck her head when cars would drive by and complain about the splinters inflicted by the wagon.

Explaining where the tractor came from requires explaining my dad and uncle's one bedrock philosophy. It was something I grew up hearing at least once a week and was forced to repeat. In its simplest form it was this: No one should pay more than $300 for a car.

In order to live by this principle, each family had to have three cars. In the ideal case, two of the cars would be running at any given time. This would allow transportation options, while the third was cycled through for repairs. Often it was the other way around, though, and one working car would have to spend its last few good miles searching for parts for the rest of the fleet.

Inevitably, my dad and uncle spent a lot of time fixing cars, and I wasn't sure they were all that good at it. Most every weekend was spent cursing carburetors, alternators, or fuel pumps. It was like a second job for both of them that they paid money to do and grumbled about the whole time. Besides fixing cars, they also spent a lot of time finding cars. That was how the tractor arrived.

My dad found someone selling a 1964 Plymouth Barracuda really cheap. When he went to look at it, he found that it didn't run but was pretty sure he knew what the problem was. The seller was willing to throw in the tractor for an extra $100 so that my dad could pull the Barracuda home. Eight hours later my mom was greeted by the sight of my dad on a tractor pulling another nonworking car. I was never sure where the wooden wagon came from. It just showed up one day.

My cousins, sisters, and I took a vote, and it was five to one in favor of using the tractor and wagon to haul the branches. Michael was against it because he just wanted to burn them. He had probably overheard my conversation with Tommy.

"Now we just have to convince our dads to let us use it and teach us to drive it," I said to everyone.

"Let me do the talking," Amy replied boldly. We found

both dads inside my uncle's house. He had bought a TV that came with a remote control, and they were both admiring it as we walked in the house.

"Watch how fast I can change the channels," said Uncle David as his thumb-clicked the little button as fast as it would go.

"You know, I'll bet this would be even more impressive if we got more than three channels." My dad laughed.

"All I really like to watch are football games and when they show movies, anyway," Uncle David responded defensively.

Amy went in and sat next to her dad.

"Can I try?" she asked, and he handed her the remote. "This is neat," she said after giving it a few clicks and handing it back.

"Daddy?" she asked.

"Yeah, honey?" he said, only half paying attention.

"Remember when you said you were going to teach me how to drive?"

"Uh-huh," he replied without taking his eyes off the TV.

"Well, I was thinking maybe you could show me how to drive the tractor to start, and then I could even use it to help out Jackson with his apple work."

Uncle David now turned his full attention to her.

"Huh? Now, what are you asking?"

"Can I learn to drive the tractor?" Amy repeated in her sweetest voice.

"And what are you planning on using it for?" asked my dad, who had now taken an interest in the conversation.

"If I can drive it, I was going to help out Jackson with his apples."

My dad and Uncle David both looked at each other. I could tell my dad wanted to say no. Uncle David, however, was thinking more about Amy, so he looked away from my dad.

"Well, I think that might be okay. You can't really go too far or too fast on a tractor," he said, looking at his daughter.

"Let's see if you can get it started first. That will prove you're ready to drive it," my dad added.

"Well, how do you start it?" Amy asked.

"We'll tell you, and you go see if you can get it running," my dad said with a little chuckle.

My dad and uncle began to describe things like "put it in neutral" and "pull the throttle all the way down" and "push in the starter button" and "push in the choke." All six kids listened closely, trying to remember all of the instructions.

"All right, you got all that?" They both laughed.

"Got it," Amy said confidently, and the rest of us kids followed her out of the house.

She led the way out to the tractor and climbed up on the bouncy metal seat while we all tried to stand behind her on the rear axle or on the running boards beside the seat.

"Okay, so what are we supposed to do first?" she asked as she grabbed the wheel.

"Put it in neutral," I replied before anyone else.

"Pull the throttle," said Lisa.

"Give it a choke," said Sam.

"Punch the starter," said Michael.

"All right, all right," Amy said, holding up her hands. "I'm not even sure what any of those things are!"

We sent the younger kids back into the house one at a time to ask where to find neutral, the throttle, choke, and starter. After fifteen minutes of confusing answers from our dads, we were ready to give something a try. We all held our breath as Amy reached toward the starter. I grabbed on to the metal wheel wells in case the thing lurched forward.

GRRR, GRRR, GRRR. The tractor made the very familiar sound of a car not starting. I knew it could have been worse, though. It could have made no sound at all.

"Maybe now a little more choke," I said.

Amy pulled the little choke lever all the way out. "All right, it's all choked. What's a choke, anyway?"

"I don't think anyone really knows. Something magic," I replied.

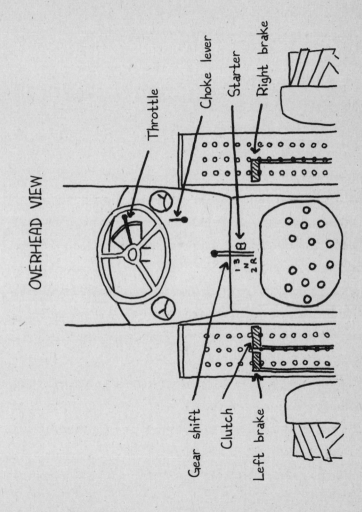

OVERHEAD VIEW

Throttle

Choke lever

Starter

Right brake

Gear shift

Clutch

Left brake

85

This time when she pushed the starter, there was a little different sound. A slightly faster *GRRR*. On the third try the engine sputtered a little, trying hard to start.

"Try half choke, half throttle, and hold the starter down for a whole minute," Michael said matter-of-factly, as if he had started tractors hundreds of times.

"Let me go ask them," I said as I climbed down and walked toward the house.

I could tell my dad and uncle were enjoying this. Trying to get them to tell me the right combination of throttle and choke was like trying to get your lunch back from a couple of school bullies. Except that most school bullies are more sympathetic. I walked back to the tractor not sure if I knew any more than when I went into the house.

"Let's try throttle down and full choke. When it starts to turn over, push the choke in and give it full gas."

Amy tried and for a second the engine sputtered and blew out a puff of exhaust.

"I think I just have to be faster," she said before trying again.

Seven attempts later the engine was running. We all jumped up and down and cheered.

"Now go forward! Go forward!" Sam yelled above the motor.

Amy looked over her shoulder at me and mouthed, "Now what?"

I ran into the house and was told about a clutch and how you had to push it in and push the gear stick into gear. I relayed this information into Amy's ear, and she pushed the clutch with her left foot, shoved the stick into position 1, and then yanked her foot up off the clutch. The tractor jumped forward a few feet. Michael flew off the back axle and the engine died. This scene repeated itself several more times, except that Sam was the only one who dared stay on the tractor with Amy.

Finally she marched toward the house, gesturing for me to follow her. We both walked into the living room, where both my uncle and dad were fighting back laughter.

"Daddy, please just come show me how to get it to move once you get it started," Amy said with a pout, looking at her dad.

"Honey, you just have to let the clutch up a little slower. You'll get it."

Just then my aunt came into the room after realizing what was happening outside. She pointed a finger at my uncle and dad. "If they get that thing started and drive it into something or someone, I am holding you two knuckleheads responsible!"

Through the windows we heard the sound of the tractor starting up. Amy and I looked at each other and hurried toward the door, followed closely by our dads.

We arrived outside just in time to see Sam behind the

wheel and the tractor moving slowly forward. He was shouting triumphantly and turning onto the dirt road in front of our houses. Very quickly, he seemed to lose his nerve. I think he realized that he didn't know how to stop. He swerved toward our house, and the tractor rammed into the '64 Barracuda my dad had parked out front. Luckily it wasn't in working condition. The tractor sputtered to a stop, and Sam jumped off, his eyes wide.

There was some mild swearing from my dad and uncle. Then my uncle started laughing, probably because none of his cars were hit. My aunt kept repeating, "I knew this was going to happen." Surprisingly, our dads agreed to show Amy and me how to drive the tractor after that, including shifting into all the gears. I think they must have felt a little guilty. By the time it got dark, we could start it, back it up, and make all kinds of turns. There was something thrilling about going down a road in third gear at ten miles per hour, the wind not exactly blowing in your hair, but at least whispering in it.

———————┐

Monday afternoon we drove the tractor and wagon into the orchard for the first time, barely missing trees as we pulled into the first row. We loaded up one and a half piles of pruned branches into the wagon, drove them out to the desolate land, and pushed them off next to some sun-bleached mounds of branches that looked like they had been there for twenty years. After two or three rows, Amy and I had gotten pretty good at turning around trees and avoiding ditches. When it got dark, we left the tractor in the orchard for the night and headed home.

When we tried to start it the next day, it wouldn't turn over. We tried every combination of choke and throttle we could think of, but nothing seemed to work. Uncle David arrived home from work before my dad, and we begged him to come help us get the engine started again. After a few attempts of his own, he jumped off the bouncy metal seat.

"I was afraid of this," he said in disgust.

"What?" Amy and I said at the same time with worried voices.

"This thing has a weird problem that we've never been able to figure out." He looked in the gas tank. "Yep. She's got plenty of gas," he said, shaking his head. He looked at me, then at Amy, then back at me. "Okay, Jackson, watch carefully. I'm going to show you what you have to do if this happens." He went to the side of the tractor where the engine was exposed and loosened a screw that was holding a flexible hose line in place. He pulled the end of the hose out from where it was connected and turned back to me.

"I don't know why, but the gas line gets clogged every so often. There must be dirt or something in it. You have to suck on this end until the line gets clear and the gas comes out." He held the line out to me. I backed up and shook my head.

"If you're going to use the tractor, you have to be able to keep it running."

I looked around. My cousins were staring at me with their eyes bugging out, watching to see if I would take the hose. I really wanted to say no, but I knew I couldn't ask anyone else to do it.

"All right," I said weakly.

I put the hose in my mouth. It tasted like a terrible combination of rubber, oil, and dirt. I closed my eyes and sucked. Suddenly my mouth filled up with a burning, awful-tasting liquid. I dropped the hose and spit. Bending over, I kept spitting to try and get the taste out of my mouth. I wanted to throw up.

When I looked up again, my uncle was putting the hose back into position.

"Very good," he said, "now just stick it back in and screw it tight."

"Is swallowing gas bad for you?" I gasped between spits.

"Oh, probably. It hasn't killed me yet," he said without much concern. Amy, Sam, and Michael looked down on me with sympathetic eyes. Amy tried the tractor again, and it started right up.

"Thanks, Daddy," she called.

My mouth tasted like gas for the next two days. We made good progress on the branches, though, especially on Saturday when Lisa and Jennifer joined us. Sam kept pestering Amy and me to teach him to drive the tractor, and finally during our afternoon Shasta break we agreed. The other kids all wanted lessons too, but we said the cutoff age was eleven, mostly because we didn't want Michael driving.

After his run-in with the Barracuda, Sam proved to be a very careful driver. He was always a little nervous and would drive so slowly, the rest of us would become impatient. Amy pulled him out of the seat before any long trips to the drop-off area.

Sam was driving the tractor into the orchard's last row with a few hours of sunlight left. Before he could pull up close to a pile of branches, the tractor sputtered a little and then the engine cut out. Instantly my stomach hurt. Amy turned to me and put her hand on my shoulder. I moved reluctantly toward the engine.

"What's he going to do?" asked Jennifer, who hadn't been around for the first gas line episode.

"You don't want to know," Michael answered solemnly.

I unscrewed the hose and pulled it out. When I put the hose in my mouth, the taste of gas came flooding back. I tried sucking very quickly then pulling the tube away so the gas wouldn't have a chance to fill up my mouth. Nothing happened. I tried sucking a little longer. Still nothing. I sucked until my cheek muscles hurt and still nothing happened.

"Amy, can you go get your dad?" I said in a defeated voice.

Ten minutes later she was back with Uncle David.

"I tried sucking really hard, but I just can't get anything to come out," I explained, holding up the tube.

Uncle David pulled off the gas cap and looked inside the tank. "That's because you don't have any gas." He stood back and looked at all of us, shook his head, and laughed. "You look like a bunch of war orphans living in the forest or something. If I had some gas, I would give you some just because you look so pitiful." We did look ragged. Almost everyone had a runny nose and scratched-up skin. Sam and Michael both had on "Hang Loose—Hawaii" T-shirts that were almost shredded. My sisters had tiny apple branches stuck in their blond hair.

My uncle thought for a moment. "Jackson, follow me. I'm going to teach you a little trick your grandpa taught me."

I followed him alone out of the orchard. He found a two-gallon gas can sitting near one of his cars and then a four-foot length of garden hose. We walked over to my house.

"I don't think your daddy would mind you borrowing a little of his gas, do you?"

We ducked behind the car my dad drove to work, and he unscrewed the gas cap. He slid the hose down the pipe that led to the gas tank.

"This is what we call siphoning. You've got to suck on the hose to start the gas flowing and then put the sucking end of the hose as low to the ground as possible. The gas will start flowing, and then you can fill up the can. Now, I know you have experience with this sort of thing"—he looked at me with a grin—"so I'm sure you can do it. Try to be as fast as you can so you swallow as little gas as possible."

I wasn't exactly sure whether he was joking or not, but I took the hose, anyway. I gave it a quick suck and then pushed it to the ground.

"You're going to have to do it a little longer than that," he said with an encouraging voice.

On the second try, my hands felt the cool gas filling the hose, but I lost my nerve and stopped sucking too soon again. On the third try, the gas poured freely. I spit and coughed as I moved the hose to the gas can.

"Get any in your mouth?" my uncle asked.

"A little. Not as much as with the tractor."

We both giggled as the can filled up, and then we pulled the hose out of the car's gas pipe. He even carried the can out to the tractor for me and helped pour it into the fuel tank.

We finished with the branches and parked the tractor back in its spot between our two houses. "So what was it my dad showed you?" asked Amy when we were alone.

"I'll teach you the next time the tractor runs out of gas," I told her. And I did. For the next six months, my dad and uncle unknowingly provided gas for the tractor. We would alternate taking it from both of their cars. We tried not to take more than two gallons at a time so they wouldn't be suspicious. I'm not sure they didn't know, however. On more than one occasion, my uncle asked my dad, in a voice that he was sure I could hear, "How's the gas gauge in your car? Mine seems to be broken since the weather's been getting hotter."

I figured we could make it up to them in free apples.

Chapter 7
WORLD'S STINKIEST SHOES

Before going to sleep on the night we finished hauling branches out of the orchard, I checked the things I
had copied out of the apple book. I couldn't help feeling proud of myself for getting the pruning done. To be
honest, I never thought we would get this far.

The apple book had not given dates for when things
should be done, but I had made a list of what should
follow what. After pruning came "preparing the soil,"
which included fertilizing. The book had talked about
a few different fertilizers. Some of them had chemical

names that sounded like they came from a secret government lab. The other kind of fertilizer was manure. I had never thought about it before, but the book said different kinds of animals made different kinds of manure. Cow manure seemed like the popular choice for apple trees.

Choosing the right fertilizer, and then getting my hands on it, was probably going to be difficult. It was something I would like to have skipped altogether, especially if manure was involved. But those trees had been ignored for five years and probably needed all the help they could get. Maybe I could use some of that clean, man-made chemical stuff if it worked. And after all that pruning work, it would be a shame if apples didn't grow.

My dad had said that there were plenty of apple farmers around, but it didn't occur to me until we started pruning that I actually knew one of them. My Sunday school teacher, Brother Brown, had a place with at least three thousand trees. I didn't think of him right away because I had never actually talked to him. He wasn't one of those teachers who bought into ideas like class discussions or nurturing learning environments. Our class was full of a dozen seventh- and eighth-graders, but after two years together I'd bet he didn't know any of our names. He was short and wrinkled with only bits of hair left on his head, and we were terrified of him. For some unspoken reason, we were sure that if we made any noise, he wouldn't be afraid to cane us, even if we were in a church class.

I watched Brother Brown carefully during our next Sunday school class, wondering if I could ask him something without getting beaten. All the other kids were looking out the window, watching a couple of dogs in the distance. Yolanda Stock's head kept bobbing up and down as she fell in and out of sleep. Brother Brown had a croaky voice that sounded like a far-off motor sputtering and choking. He started by talking about Daniel in the lion's den and then meandered lifelessly into his favorite topic, the Sermon on the Mount.

When class ended, all the other kids fled. I waited around in front of the door, blocking Brother Brown's exit. He had his head down and almost walked into me.

"Brother Brown, I just wanted to say that I liked your lesson about Daniel . . . and the Sermon on the Mount too."

He kept his head down, looking on either side of my feet for an escape route.

"I hate to bother you here at church, but you're the only person who can help me."

He raised his head a little. His face and hands were not only wrinkled; they looked like they had been baked in an oven until there was a tough, brown shell around them.

"I was hoping you could give me some advice on fertilizer."

He leveled his head and looked right at me. "Like what?"

"Like do you ever use any of those chemical types?"

"Nah, I can't keep track of all of 'em. Stick with the natural stuff when I need it."

"Like manure?"

"Yep."

"Well, where can I get some?"

"Just follow your nose, son."

And with that he squeezed his way around me and was gone. I would have liked to have asked him more questions, like how many cows it took to fertilize one tree. I assumed three hundred trees meant something like three hundred cows.

There were a few places up and down the main road that looked like they had those kinds of cow numbers, including a couple of dairies. The smelliest of the dairies was about a mile from our house. On a hot summer day, if the wind was blowing just right, you could catch a whiff of it even inside. My mom would scrunch up her nose and say, "I wish they would clean up that place! It's not right that we should have to smell it too."

The dairy happened to be on our bus route, so I got to see it every school day. Five or six kids would get off the bus near there. On Monday after school, I held my breath and followed them.

Amy looked at me with an almost frightened expression as I walked past her.

"I'll see you in half an hour or so," I said to her quickly before my exit.

Looking around, it was hard to tell where humans would actually work at the dairy. There were a few wooden buildings with holes in the sides that looked like they were about to collapse. Mostly there were cows inside weak-looking wooden fences. They were standing very close together. Most of them were black and white, but halfway up their bodies they were covered in manure that was a disgusting brown-green. I wondered why they didn't all just push against those fences and get out. They all just stood there, though, chewing with blank expressions on their faces. Maybe cows liked being together like this. And when it came to making lots of manure, these were definitely the right kind of cows.

I wandered cautiously over to the biggest of the buildings. I didn't see any movement and was afraid to go inside, so I started shouting.

"Hello! Is anybody there? I need to talk to someone about manure. Hello!"

A short man with a buzzed haircut came walking out. He was wearing a filthy brown jumpsuit. Like the cows, he had a coating of manure almost halfway up his body.

"You the one callin' out?" he asked, with a big toothy smile. His teeth were perfectly straight and very white against the brown jumpsuit and surroundings.

"Uh, yeah, it was me. I live down the road about a mile." I pointed toward my house. "I need to talk with someone about manure."

He put his hand out to shake. "Jerry Wheeler. If there's anything I'm an expert on, it's manure." His hand was just as dirty as his jumpsuit. I hesitated, then swallowed hard and shook it.

"So whatcha wanna know?"

"I've got this orchard I'm trying to take care of. Used to be Mr. Nelson's—Jack Nelson's."

"Oh yeah, I know the place."

"So, anyway, I got a bunch of trees I need to fertilize, and Brother Brown, you know the man with the big orchard, he says manure's the best thing for 'em."

"You're takin' care of that Nelson place all by yourself?"

"Well, me and my cousins and sisters. But I'm kinda in charge."

He gave a whistle. "That's a pretty big job at your age. Aren't you supposed to be havin' fun and worrying about school and what girls you like?"

I blushed a little. "I guess. But now we've been working on it for a couple months so we want to make sure the trees make apples."

"Only sounds fair." He nodded. "Wish I had some hard-workin' boys like you around here." He gave me another big smile.

"So is there any way I could have some of your manure for the trees?"

"Okay with me, but I better check with my pop first. Hey, Pop!" he yelled loudly. "Hey, Pop, come on out here!"

Another short man walked out of the building. He wore the same brown coveralls and had the same buzzed haircut. He had a pot belly and looked about thirty years older than Jerry. Jerry told him what I wanted, and then he put his hand out to me. "Hoppy Wheeler. Glad to meet you."

I shook his hand and said, "Hoppy?" without thinking.

"Funny name, isn't it? You can blame my brothers for it," he said with a laugh. "As you can see, we make two things around here, milk and manure. Probably better known for the manure, though."

I laughed. "Do you have any extra I could use?"

"I'd say a hard workin' little farmer like you could have all he wants."

"Really?"

"'Course I'm sure you won't forget us when those apples are ready, right?" he said with a wink. "You got a way to haul the stuff?"

"Yeah, we've got a tractor with a wagon."

"You see that big pile at the end of the fences? Feel free to load it up down there."

I thanked them both a few times, and they slapped me on the back, still laughing about me being a little farmer. I ran the mile back home and found Sam and Michael watching *Tom and Jerry* on TV. Amy was holding the phone with its cord wound around her and chattering away with one of her friends.

"Okay, guys, I'm back," I said loudly while trying to catch my breath. "Were you worried about me?"

"I liked having you gone," said Michael, still staring at the TV. I waited for him to laugh, but he didn't.

I looked over at Amy and made a sign that I had something to tell everyone. She gave me a sour look, rolled her eyes, and started easing her way out of the phone conversation. I waited until she hung up and then said, "Sorry to spoil everyone's party, but I've been making arrangements for our next big job."

"What is it?" asked Sam.

"I'll tell you after we make some changes to the wagon," I said, trying to sound mysterious. "So, who's ready?"

Amy moved grudgingly to turn off the TV. Michael,

who hadn't been paying attention, jerked up and whined, "Hey, what's going on?"

The three of them followed me out to the tractor and wagon parked between our houses. "We need to figure out a way to add some sides to this wagon so it can hold some stuff."

"What kind of stuff?" Amy asked suspiciously.

"You'll see. But first I guess we need some boards that we could attach to the sides. Any ideas?"

Everyone's eyes moved toward the clubhouse a few feet away that Amy and I had built when we were ten. We had had grand designs but ended up with a collection of weatherworn boards and wood scraps held together with rusty nails at crooked angles. The whole thing collapsed after a couple of swings with a hammer. We put some of the biggest boards against the side of the wagon and nailed them into place.

"How strong does it have to be?" asked Sam as he pulled on a board, causing it to bend easily.

"I think a lot stronger than that," I replied in a discouraged voice.

My dad came walking up while we were discussing alternate designs.

"Don't you kids have a farm to run? What are you doing hanging around here?"

"We're trying to add some sides to the wagon so it can hold things better," I answered.

He looked at the boards we had nailed into place, wiggling them back and forth.

"This has got to be the shoddiest piece of work I've ever seen. Looks like it was done by a bunch of ding-a-ling kids. Where'd you learn to build?"

"Nowhere. That's the problem. I guess our dads never taught us anything useful like that," I said. I knew I was pushing my luck with that last statement. After saying it, I hoped he was in a good mood.

"Oh really?" he said, looking at me. "Well, if you can go convince your mother not to cook that fish for dinner like she's planning, I'll give you a lesson better than any school."

I ran into the house to find my mom. She was unwrapping some fish just like my dad had said.

"Mom, will you please do me a huge favor?" I asked very seriously.

"What is it, honey?" she asked, looking concerned.

"Okay, promise you won't laugh, but it's something about school and trying to get good grades."

"Okay, okay, just tell me."

"I've got this really big history test coming up on Thursday morning that is like a big part of our grade for the semester. I know that fish is supposed to be good for your brain, so could we please have it on Wednesday to help me with my test?" I looked up at her with begging eyes.

"Of course, sweetheart! I didn't even know it could help you like that. Maybe we should have it more often. Tonight I'll just throw something else together."

When I got back, my dad had already torn off the extra boards from the wagon.

"Mom's cooking something else," I announced.

"Really? Good boy!" Dad said happily. "Now, how high do you want the walls on this thing?"

"Say, about two feet."

"Hmm. We'll have to build some kind of braces to give them some strength."

Once he got started, he became obsessed with making the walls sturdy and uniform. He didn't finish until Tuesday night, and all my cousins and I did was hand

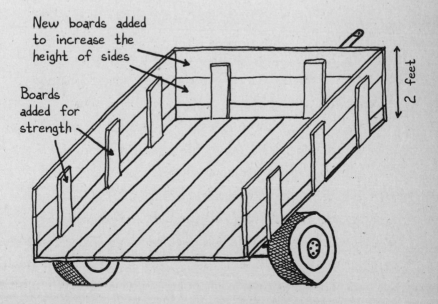

New boards added to increase the height of sides

Boards added for strength

2 feet

him tools and nails and hold boards straight. In the end, it looked pretty good, with walls on the sides and front and the back left open. I hoped he wouldn't tear it all apart when he got served fish on Wednesday.

———————

After school on Wednesday, I gathered everyone around the tractor and told them about my trip to the Wheeler dairy. There was a look of horror on every face when I told them we were going to use the wagon to haul manure from there to the orchard and then spread it around the trees. Amy was the first to speak.

"First, let me just say I can't believe you actually went and talked to them. And second, I know I said I would help and everything, but this is just too much. I can't be involved in any manure work. I'll do something else, but I can't go with you." Her face was more determined than I had ever seen it.

"Listen, if we don't fertilize, I'm not sure we're going to get good apples. I don't want to do it either." I turned to Sam. "Sam, how about you?"

"I . . . I . . . don't know. Are we going to get really dirty and smelly? I don't think my mom will like that."

"You can drive the tractor wherever we go."

"Okay, I'll do it," he said grudgingly.

I turned to Michael, who looked much more negative.

"How about you, Michael?

"No way. If Amy doesn't have to, then neither do I."

"You can have a pop every day you help. Even week-days."

The power Shasta had over Michael was amazing, because after considering it for a few seconds, he said, "All right."

Amy agreed to stay behind and start chopping the weeds that surrounded all the trees. It made sense to us that weeds shouldn't be getting any of the manure meant for the trees.

I grabbed some shovels and an old tarp my dad sometimes used for covering up cars when it rained. I put the tarp in the bottom of the wagon, figuring it would be best to keep manure off as much of the wagon as possible—if we planned on ever using it again.

Sam, Michael, and I made the slow drive down the road with Sam at the wheel. He was even more nervous than usual because cars kept whizzing past us, but we ended up safely next to Hoppy's manure pile. It hadn't rained for a while and the pile seemed to be fairly old, so fortunately the manure was pretty dry. We started out by standing at the bottom of the pile and shoveling manure up and into the wagon. My back and shoulders instantly hurt.

Sam climbed onto the manure pile and started shoveling manure down toward us. "This is a lot easier, guys. Come up here," he said.

I looked down at my shoes, shook my head, and

climbed up. After what seemed like two hours, Sam was driving slowly out to the road, leaving a cloud of swirling manure dust behind us.

When we reached the orchard, Sam pulled the tractor into the first row of trees and Michael and I stood in the wagon, shoveling manure over the sides. We weren't really sure how much to throw at any given spot and just kept working until the ground and weeds under each tree had a thin coating. Shoveling out took less time than shoveling in, but we only had enough manure for one row. My back was pinched in pain and my hands covered in filthy blisters as we spread the last shovelfuls.

"Kill the motor and let's leave it here tonight," I said to Sam.

Amy came walking over to us.

"You look terrible, and you smell just like, well, you know what," she said, laughing.

"Thanks, we know! And thanks a lot for helping," Sam replied angrily.

"You better follow me. There's no way you're getting in the house looking like that."

We followed Amy to the yard of their house and stood on the little lawn as she made us strip down to our underwear and sprayed us off. The water was freezing, and I ran hard back to my house. I met my mom at the door, dripping wet and holding my clothes.

"What do you think you're doing without any clothes on?" she demanded.

"Just finished some fertilizing and, trust me, you'd hate it worse with my clothes on," I said through chattering teeth. I left my wet shoes outside, put some dry clothes on, and took Michael's Shasta over to him.

—————⌐

Since I only had one pair of tennis shoes, I had to wear my dress shoes to school the next day. I usually only wore them to church and told my friends at school that "my cousin said these are coming into style," because I didn't want to have to explain the manure.

Later that day Sam, Michael, and I were on our way back toward the dairy, all of our shoes still damp. We were dressed in the very worst clothes we could find and wore handkerchiefs to cover our noses and mouths and gloves to cover our blisters.

When we pulled into the dairy, Jerry greeted us with a big grin. We slowed down as he motioned to us.

"Back already, huh? You must really like this stuff."

"Yeah, we only got one row done yesterday. Got twenty-nine to go. Loading it up takes forever. I don't know how long we can last," I yelled over the hum of the tractor while shaking my head.

"Tell you what, I'll go grab the front-loader and help you boys out."

"Really? It's not too much trouble?"

"Nah. I like seeing some people once in a while. Otherwise it's just me and these stupid cows."

He walked toward the end of the pen full of cows and started up a dirty-looking front-loading tractor used to push piles of manure around. We pulled our wagon over to our original loading point. Jerry drove the scoop of the front-loader into the huge pile, backed up, and dumped it into the wagon. Its axle shuddered. We gave a little cheer and waved to Jerry.

"Any time you need a load, just come and get me!" he shouted over the engines of both tractors.

Not having to fill the wagon by hand, we were able to finish two rows that night and were much less tired, but still filthy. Amy was waiting with the hose when we were done, and we each took our turn getting sprayed without saying a word.

———⟶

On the weekend Lisa and Jennifer joined Amy in cutting down weeds around the trees. I didn't even bother asking them if they were willing to help with the manure.

We made good time on Saturday, and whenever we arrived at the dairy and called for Jerry, he came hustling out of his run-down building. He laughed and joked with us like we were the highlight of his whole day. We brought him a cold Shasta, and he drank it down without stopping to wipe off the top.

It was a pretty warm day for early April, and midway through the afternoon my mom came marching into the orchard. We were spreading a load on one of the rows.

"What do you think you're doing?" she yelled.

"We're fertilizing, like I told you," I yelled back.

"Do you know what this smells like?"

"Pretty well, yes."

"And look at you, you're all filthy! You're going to get sick."

"We've got to do it, Mom. It's part of the job. I don't like it either."

I guess she hadn't really understood what we were doing until she saw half the orchard now covered in manure. Her face filled with disgust as she realized we had hauled a part of the dairy to her and dumped it right in front of her house. She gave a scream of frustration as she stomped back home.

The next day she tried to persuade my dad that we shouldn't be allowed to continue. He thought the whole situation was funny and simply said, "Well, honey, you know being a farmer is not all glamour. It's about connecting with the soil too."

Mrs. Nelson seemed just as revolted as my mom. She caught my attention one day when we were returning from a dairy run. I shouted for Sam to stop the tractor so she could talk to us.

"Hi, Mrs. Nelson," I called out.

As she walked closer, her eyes became bigger and she turned her head away.

"Jackson, what is that smell?" she said as she grimaced.

"We're fertilizing, the natural way."

"Do you have to?"

"If we want a lot of apples. Didn't Mr. Nelson ever fertilize like this?"

"Oh, no! I would never have let him back in the house!"

She marched away in a huff. I smiled, thinking that if Mr. Nelson had never bothered to fertilize, maybe he had never gotten all he could out of the trees. Maybe we would have an edge. We had better.

———————

We finished with the manure work on the second Saturday after we had started. When we pulled away from the dairy, a very small part of me was sad to wave goodbye to Jerry, who had been so good to us.

No matter how many times I washed my shoes after that, they never stopped smelling. They were only good for working in the orchard from then on. They were only Fastbacks, some generic brand my mom had bought, but I was still tired of wearing my dress shoes everywhere. I asked my mom if I could get next year's school shoes early so I wouldn't have to wear my dress shoes anymore. I was hoping to get some high-tops because some of the kids at school were starting to wear them.

"It's your own fault you ruined the pair you had, so you can wait until next fall," she told me.

She was clearly paying me back for the smell that was now always there when you walked out of the house.

I hid my dad's tarp in the orchard, buried under some weeds and dirt. That, too, was never going to be the same. I hoped he would forget about it or think it had blown away.

I knew I owed Sam and Michael everything if those trees ever produced apples. There's something about standing knee deep in a pile of manure together that makes you feel close to someone, and I was feeling very emotional as the three of us hosed off the tractor after our last run. "Guys, I just want to say that was the worst experience of my life. I don't know two other people who would have helped with it. You're, like, the best friends I have," I blurted out.

"I'm never doing it again," said Michael sharply.

"Yeah, that's for sure. I don't think I ever even want to talk about this again. Let's just keep it all between us," said Sam, holding his soggy shoes.

We nodded our heads in agreement. I called to the girls, who were walking out of the orchard, and motioned them over. Sam and Michael sprayed them with the hose as soon as they were in range.

"Hey, Amy, here's a little taste of what we got," yelled Michael as he drenched her.

Chapter 8
SAVE THE BLOSSOMS

It was early April. I hadn't noticed it while shoveling manure, but on close inspection the trees were beginning to look a different color. Up and down their reddish-brown branches, little specks of green were breaking out.

Sam, Michael, and I had joined Amy cutting down the weeds poking out from the manure layer surrounding each tree. It was nice to be listening to the radio again, even if we had to hear "Billie Jean" and "Beat It" twice an hour. And compared with being covered in manure, I felt so fresh, it was like working in a bank or department store. Amy and my sisters had finished work on three rows and had piled the biggest weeds in the space between the rows where the tractor would usually drive. The cleared trees looked starkly clean without the tangle of weeds surrounding their trunks. All that chopping had also mixed the manure into the soil, coloring it with yellow and green clumps.

"This looks like someone knows what they're doing," I said to Amy.

"Well, we don't, really. And once all these stupid trees are done, I'm never doing it again," she replied quickly.

I held back a grin. "I still think it looks good."

———

The boys and I copied Amy as much as we could for the rest of the week. We could only find three hoes scattered around our yards, so I used a shovel to dig up the biggest weeds and willow trees that had begun to grow throughout the orchard.

Something was definitely happening to the apple trees. Every day we rolled into spring, little red-green buds began to appear and grow fatter and fatter, bulging with life. When I woke up one Saturday morning, they had exploded over the entire orchard into tiny pink blossoms. I ran through the orchard checking all the trees. Every one of them was blooming. The pale pink popcorn against the dark apple wood was stunningly beautiful. Although I had lived my whole life next to those trees, I had never noticed before.

I was stroking some blossom petals when the other kids showed up in the orchard. "Well, what do you think?" I asked.

"About what?" asked Amy.

"The blossoms. Just look around!"

"Yeah, they're pretty."

"And do you know what this means? The trees are alive. They're going to make apples. Every blossom is an apple."

"I'm not sure that's right, but what are you getting so excited about, anyway?" asked Lisa, unimpressed.

"Isn't it nice to know that all our work so far wasn't wasted?"

"But this is what trees do with or without us," Lisa replied simply.

Everyone seemed more interested in who was going to use one of the three hoes we had for cutting weeds. I was still poking blossoms when Amy told me I needed to go see if Mrs. Nelson had any more hoes in her shed. I knew at least Mrs. Nelson would gush over the blossoms, so I yanked off a branch covered in pink and headed for her house.

"Good morning, Mrs. Nelson!" I said happily when she answered her door.

She looked at me and sniffed the air. "Why, you don't smell at all this morning," she said in surprise.

"Thank you," I replied. "We're done with fertilizing. I brought you something." I held up the blossom-covered branch.

She blinked a few times as if it were blinding her, and then she reached for it. "Oh, I didn't realize it was already time. They're just as beautiful as I remember." She sniffed at the blossoms and caressed the petals. "Oh, Jackson, don't you think they're the prettiest things?"

"Yeah, I do. But I'm not sure everyone cares like we do," I said, but she wasn't really listening.

"Why don't you come out and walk through the orchard?" I suggested.

"Oh yes, I'll do that. Just give me a minute to get ready," said Mrs. Nelson excitedly.

"While I'm waiting, can I have another look around the tool shed?" I asked.

"Go ahead," she replied, and went back into her house to change her clothes.

I cracked open the dark shed and began looking for tools that could be used for weed chopping. I noticed the tangle of hoses again and a big pile of bent aluminum tubes that I couldn't figure out. I didn't find more hoes, but I did find a couple of what people call "weed whackers." At the end of a wooden handle was a sharp metal blade. When you swung it back and forth, you could take out weeds with every swing.

I met Mrs. Nelson coming out of her door. I let her lead the way toward the nearest row of trees. She picked her way gingerly through the weeds bordering the orchard while I hung back, taking practice swings along the way with the weed whackers. "How are you feeling lately, Mrs. Nelson? Any healthier?" I asked, trying to make conversation.

"That doctor of mine says I don't have cancer after all." She sighed.

"Well, that's good news." I was surprised that she didn't sound happier about the diagnosis.

"I suppose. Looks like I'll be around longer than I thought. Wish I felt stronger, though." She had reached the nearest tree and stood next to it letting out *ooh*s and *ah*s over the blossoms.

I fished for compliments by pointing out the pruned branches and fertilized soil, but she ignored me.

"These flowers certainly are glorious. The best thing about the whole orchard. I wouldn't care if there weren't any apples, as long as I could see this every spring."

That wasn't quite the response I was looking for. In fact, what she was saying made me feel a little discouraged. I liked the blossoms, too, but come on; the apples were the important things.

She inspected a few more trees and then said, "I'm glad I made it one more year. But all the excitement's worn me out. I've got to go sit down."

I probably should have walked her back to her house, but instead I let her stumble back alone while I returned to Amy and the others.

Amy had been watching me and Mrs. Nelson but didn't say anything when I walked up. She grabbed the weed whackers and insisted that I use the shovel I was usually stuck with. Sam and Michael took the weed whackers and started swinging enthusiastically. At first we all worked around the same tree until Michael came within inches of hitting Amy with a wild swing.

"Are you trying to kill me, you idiot? You almost hit me in the head!" she screamed.

"It's not my fault you're so close!" Michael yelled back.

"Why don't you go on to the next tree, then!" And with that, she split us up into teams of boys and girls. The boys were supposed to stay one tree ahead of the girls and concentrate on the largest weeds. After ten minutes of ducking Sam's and Michael's swings, I told Amy I was moving an extra tree ahead.

It was amazing how fast we worked when pacing each other. The boys constantly accused the girls of being too slow, and the girls replied that we were sloppy and, of course, dangerous. We hadn't shared a Shasta together for a couple of weeks, since the girls wouldn't come near us during manure days. During breaks it was nice to sit down together again and feel the spring sun on our arms and faces. Bees had begun to move from blossom to blossom, and it made the whole place feel full of energy. When we decided to quit working, I grabbed a branch full of flowers for my mom, thinking she would like them as much as Mrs. Nelson.

"Look what I picked for you, Mom," I said proudly when I found her in the kitchen.

"What is that supposed to be?" she asked, looking at the branch.

"It's a branch of apple blossoms. I thought it would be nice to put in a vase, kind of like flowers."

"Hmm . . . thanks, sweetie." She pulled off a stem from the branch and placed it in a jar of water. "I just hope your father doesn't get the idea he can give me a branch off of a tree and call it 'flowers.'"

I cradled what remained of the branch and turned to go to my room.

"I hope for your sake it doesn't freeze and kill all your blossoms this year," she added casually.

"What? What do you mean?" I asked in a panicky voice.

"You know. If we get a late frost and it wipes out all the fruit for the year."

"No, I don't know! How does something like that happen?"

"Well, if it drops below freezing, I guess the blossoms just die before they turn to apples. Happens to the peaches and apricots too."

I looked at her in terror, but she kept her back to me while she talked, oblivious to the havoc she was wreaking inside my head.

"How do you know all this? When has it ever happened?" I demanded.

"I don't know personally about it, but everyone around here always talks about whether the fruit trees are going to freeze. I think it happened last year."

I backed out of the kitchen and stumbled back to my room as if I'd been kicked in the gut. I put my little branch of blossoms on the windowsill next to my bed and stared at it. Had I read anything about this? I couldn't quite remember. I hadn't written anything down about it. That worthless book. It was probably written about Florida apples or someplace that never got cold.

I stared at the ceiling for a while and then went to talk to my dad, who was watching *The Love Boat* on TV. "Have they said what the weather's going to be like tonight?" I asked.

"Tonight? Why, you got a date or something?" He grinned.

"No. It's really important for the trees," I said seriously.

"I think the weather guy said thirty-six degrees for a low in Farmington."

I felt momentary relief but could hardly get to sleep that night because I felt so cold. I woke up still worried about freezing trees. All morning my mom kept saying, "Stop biting your lip, that's not going to help anything." She always nagged that I bit my lip when I was worried.

I was still obsessing on thirty-two degrees Fahrenheit while sitting in Sunday school. I hadn't paid much attention to Brother Brown. ". . . and Jesus taught we could pray about anything, no matter where we are," he droned dully.

Suddenly, the anxiety became too much. I bit my lip and then started speaking without even raising my hand. "Brother Brown, is it true that if the temperature goes below freezing, it can kill apple blossoms?"

He looked at me as if part of the roof had fallen on his head. He paused, blinked hard, and said impatiently, "Uh, yes, that's true."

"Well, what are you supposed to do about it?"

"Not much you can do," he replied irritably in his croaky voice.

"What about praying? Does that help?"

He paused uncomfortably. I would have thought that a Sunday school teacher was supposed to automatically say yes. He shifted from side to side and looked down.

He finally raised his head and looked me square in the eyes. I waited for a deep, profound answer. Slowly he said, "Sometimes." The wrinkles on his face looked tired and deep.

We stared at each other wordlessly. I bit my lip and asked, "Well, do you pray for your trees?" My voice cracked a little on the last words.

This time he didn't hesitate and said more strongly, "Yes."

I finally became aware of all the other faces in the room staring at me. In our class, hearing a voice other than Brother Brown's had been the equivalent of a bomb going off, and everyone was now sitting up in their chairs.

"Sorry for interrupting," I blurted out, and slouched down as far as possible.

———

That afternoon my family was having dinner with my cousins. I gathered all the kids around and told them I had something very important to announce. After discussing the freezing possibility that had been confirmed by a "reliable source," I told them they all had to pray to keep the apples safe.

"I've already been praying for the trees," announced Lisa self-righteously. "But I guess I can include something about them not freezing."

"Should we really be praying to control the weather,

though? What if someone else needs it to be cold?" asked Sam.

"Maybe we could pray for it to be warm just around the orchard, and it could be whatever temperature everywhere else," offered Michael.

"Listen, just pray for the apples to survive. That's all he wants," said Amy impatiently.

When we sat down to dinner, I asked if I could say the blessing on the food. The adults acted surprised but readily agreed. I bowed my head seriously and began.

"Our Father which art in heaven. We are thankful for the springtime and for the new blossoms on the trees, especially the apple trees. We are thankful they are still alive after the winter. Please let them stay warm so their apples can live, just anything above thirty-two degrees. Please don't let the work of your children be wasted . . . And bless this food. Amen."

All the adults were looking at each other with crooked grins on their faces when I opened my eyes.

"What?" I asked loudly.

"Nothing, honey," said my mom. "That was sweet."

I was fourteen years old, and I wasn't sure I had really meant anything I had prayed before. I knew I wasn't supposed to think about prayers as magic or wishing or anything, but I guess that's what it had felt like in the past. That night when I was alone, I prayed like I was lost, begging for a way home.

The next three days it rained and even sprinkled during the night. It made working outside so muddy that we called it quits after an hour. Everyone was thrilled. I was thrilled it had stayed above forty degrees.

———————

On Thursday morning the sky was a deep blue, and the moment I stepped outside I could tell the temperature had dropped. We were able to get back into the orchard that afternoon, but I was terrified at what might happen during the night.

"What do they say the temperature will be?" I asked my dad later, not daring to look at the TV.

He saw my worried face and hesitated. "They said thirty-one, son, but I don't want you to get all worked up. They're hardly ever right, and we're usually a couple of degrees warmer than Farmington."

I tried to sleep but kept popping out of bed to pace the floor between my door and window. Every hour or so, I tiptoed into the kitchen and called the phone number that reported the time and temperature. At 3:30 a.m., the voice said thirty-two degrees. I prayed some more. I felt absolutely helpless. I wished I had three hundred blankets or tarps to wrap around the trees. Why had we picked up those branches? We could have made bonfires to warm up the whole place.

My mom had to come and wake me up the next morning, and I could feel I had bit my lip raw. At school

I could barely keep my head off the desk. When I got home, I scanned the local paper looking for the overnight temperature. It listed thirty-one.

"What's wrong?" asked Amy as I joined my cousins in the orchard. "You look like you're going to throw up."

"Nothing!" I said, trying my best to appear cheerful. I didn't want everyone else worrying and giving up. For the rest of Friday and all of Saturday, I kept fairly quiet and a couple of trees ahead of the others, knocking manure off the biggest weeds and then attacking them with my shovel. I was thinking of what I would say to everyone if I had to break the news about a frozen crop. There had been more and more blossoms blooming every day, so that every tree looked like it was coated in pink snow. I had no idea if this was a good or bad sign.

It was late afternoon, and the others were discussing whether or not you could be killed by a bee's sting as bees buzzed around our heads. ". . . I'm just telling you what my teacher said. Some people are extra allergic, and even one sting can kill them," stated Lisa matter-of-factly.

"But bees don't sting as bad as black widows, and even they won't kill you," replied Sam.

Amy wasn't paying attention and was singing along to Duran Duran on the radio.

"Why don't we call it a day?" I announced.

"Really? Already?" asked Lisa.

"Why? Aren't we going to finish the other trees?" asked Jennifer.

"Yeah, but you've been working so hard that I think you deserve a break," I explained.

"Sounds good to me," said Amy, throwing down her hoe but giving me a squinting stare.

Something in me couldn't go on anymore without knowing.

——⌐

Before church the next day, I wandered through the orchard examining branches. They were still covered in blossoms, but I didn't know the difference between a live blossom and a frozen one. I shook a few trees to see if anything fell off. The pink petals hung on stubbornly.

As soon as Brother Brown came into our Sunday school class, I got up and walked toward him. "Did they make it?" I asked very seriously. I could see he instantly knew what I was talking about. I could feel the worry written all over my face.

The side of his mouth raised up as if involuntarily starting to grin. "Well, I think they pulled through."

"Really?" I replied breathlessly. I wanted to shake his hand or hug him. Instead, I sat in the seat closest to where he was standing.

——⌐

The temperature rose steadily after that week, rarely dipping into the thirties again. The blossoms eventually fell off the trees in a great shower that covered the ground in pink. They left tiny round balls behind that were the start of apples.

Their appearance made the orchard feel more serious, as if spring's allusions were over and the real business of growing had begun. Our work felt more serious too. If the trees and weather hadn't cooperated, we could have quit then and there. My sisters and cousins would have felt gypped, but I wouldn't get all the blame. Now the expectation of a payoff began to grow with the apples. There was no going back, and someday soon my promises were going to come due.

Chapter 9
WATER, THE FREE AND DANGEROUS KIND

The New Mexico state flower is the yucca. A yucca probably has more in common with a cactus than it does with an everyday flower. It grows long, needle-sharp leaves that stick out like a porcupine's quills. From the middle of these a tall stem grows, decorated with yellow petals.

When you grow up in New Mexico, just like the yucca, you rarely have access to much water. If left alone, most of the land would look like our plot of desolation—dirt, rocks, and tough weeds. You start seeing the world in browns and reds.

The area surrounding our house was mostly those colors except right near the front door. My mom had planted a little patch of grass she called her "touch of civilization." It was only about fifteen by fifteen square feet, but my dad wouldn't let it get any bigger because it had to be watered with city water that came from the tap. We were repeatedly reminded 'that they charged by the gallon for that stuff'.

Not all of the area around Farmington was desolate. The San Juan River brought some of it to life. People had been irrigating for decades by pulling water out of the river with canals. Wide swaths of the valley between the river's plateaus were green with fields of alfalfa, beans, and corn.

The nearest canal to our house was on the opposite side of the road that led to Farmington—State Highway 550. One thing the library's apple book had made clear was that an apple tree needed lots of water. I knew that Mr. Nelson must have used water from that canal if he had ever gotten anything to grow, but I had no idea how he'd done it. In fact, since I could walk, I had always been warned to stay away from the canal. In my mother's eyes, it was nothing but a baby killer that could sweep away and drown her kids.

As the weather grew warmer, I knew we had to get some serious water on the trees. This meant figuring out the canal and irrigation. I went through my usual progression of adult advisors.

Mrs. Nelson simply said, "I know my husband used to go across the road to turn the water on. He used to always wear big rubber boots and take a shovel."

My dad said, "If you can figure it out, let me know 'cause I'd like to use some on this yard. Something besides these weeds might class things up a little."

———————

Again I found myself in Sunday school staring at Brother Brown. After the close call with the blossoms, our joint worrying had brought us together somehow. At least I felt that way about him. It was still unclear how he felt about me.

I cornered him after class, blocking his way to the door. "So how are your trees doing?" I began.

"Fine," he answered, trying not to look at me.

"Brother Brown, when is it time to start watering them? You know, with irrigation?"

He seemed a bit amused. "Is there water in the canal?"

"Ummm, I don't know."

"Well, you can't water without water."

"When there's water in it, do you think I could come watch you, you know, irrigate?"

He thought about this a long time. "We'll see when there's water."

I thought that sounded pretty hopeful. A "we'll see" was getting pretty close to a "maybe," and with my dad at least, that wasn't far from an "okay."

———————

After school the next day, I jumped off the bus and announced to everyone, "I'm going over to check the canal. Who wants to come with me?"

Sam's and Michael's eyebrows went up. Lisa's eyebrows went down. Amy kept walking toward home. After assuring Lisa that we were on official orchard business and she shouldn't tell Mom, Sam, Michael, and I dodged traffic and crossed the road.

We climbed the embankment that hid the canal. The canal banks were thickly crowded with little trees and weeds, so it was hard to see if there was water flowing or not. We inched our way down the bank through the screen of plants until we reached a dry bottom. No water yet. Sam and Michael began wandering down the length of the canal.

"We better go, you guys," I called out. "We don't want to be down here if the water turns on." My accumulated years of warning had begun to make me nervous.

———————

We repeated our canal inspection on Tuesday and still found it dry. On Wednesday, however, muddy water was flowing six feet deep and ten feet wide.

"It's on! It's on!" I yelled at my cousins.

"Now what?" asked Sam.

"I dunno. We're going to need some serious help."

That night I grabbed the phone book and turned the pages toward the BROWNs.

"Mom, do you know Brother Brown's name?" I called to her.

"You mean your Sunday school teacher?"

"Uh-huh."

"I think it's Jess or Jessie."

I looked through the list. There was only one Jess. I read out the number to my mom.

"Does that sound right?"

"How should I know?" she replied.

I grabbed the phone, untwisted the long cord, and dialed. I half hoped it was the wrong number.

"Hello?" said a woman's voice on the other end.

"Um, is Brother Brown there?"

There was a pause, then, "Yes, I'll get him." It seemed like a whole minute went by.

"Yeah, hello?" said a recognizable, croaky voice.

"Hello, Brother Brown, this is Jackson Jones from your Sunday school class." I paused, but he didn't say anything. "I saw that the canal water got turned on today, and I was wondering if I could come over and watch you irrigate. Like we talked about."

There was a long silence. "When would you want to come?" he finally asked.

"Anytime that's good for you. Oh, wait, no, I guess it would have to be after school. Say, four o'clock."

"Well . . . I guess so. Be here tomorrow."

"Thanks. Thanks a lot. I'll see you tomorrow."

I hung up the phone excitedly. I ran and told Amy and the boys about the special training and how I thought we should all be a part of it.

"How are we supposed to get there?" asked Amy.

"Ride the tractor," I suggested. She groaned, but the boys liked the idea. I also told Lisa and Jennifer that we had to make a special exception and they needed to come along even if it was a school night.

"Think of it as kind of like a class. Or a field trip. Whatever you feel best about," I explained.

"I don't feel good about either one," grumbled Lisa.

———————

Amy drove the tractor the next day because she said it was better than riding in the wagon. We pulled up into Brother Brown's yard and saw him walking toward us. I jumped out of the wagon while everyone piled out behind me. "Brother Brown," I called cheerfully, "I brought my whole work crew with me."

Amy gave me a dirty look while Brother Brown inspected us and grunted a little. He was wearing blue bib overalls, and he looked more relaxed than he ever did at church.

"Let's go, then," he said, and gestured toward the nearest trees.

We followed him in single file, walking past a large, brightly painted green tractor.

"I like your tractor, Brother Brown. It's a John Deere right?" called out Sam.

Brother Brown turned his head slightly to see who had spoken but didn't say a word in return. We tunneled through a part of his orchard. The trees were about the same size as ours, but the rows much longer so that when you were in the middle of one, you began to lose your sense of direction. We emerged near the highway and then followed Brother Brown across. He climbed the canal embankment and found what looked like a steering wheel attached to a long screw. The screw ran down into a cement wall built into the side of the canal. Brother Brown began turning the steering wheel, which raised a sheet of metal built into the cement.

"Uh, whatcha doin'?" I called to him from a little way up the canal's bank.

"Gotta open the ditch," he said, and kept turning.

With each twist of the wheel, the metal sheet rose higher and water began rushing into a smaller ditch perpendicular to the canal. When the gate was all the

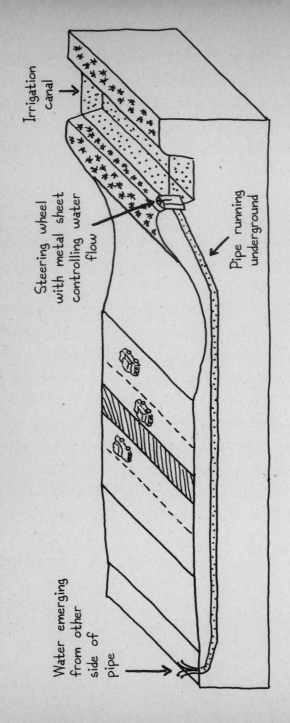

Irrigation canal

Steering wheel with metal sheet controlling water flow

Pipe running underground

Water emerging from other side of pipe

way up, a healthy stream of water had filled the ditch, flowing toward the road and disappearing.

"Where's the water going?" I asked Brother Brown.

"Pipe under the road carries it to the other side," he said as he climbed the canal bank and started walking toward his orchard.

"Does everyone have a gate and a wheel like that?"

"Everyone who can get water."

"How can I find the one for our orchard?"

"Better start lookin'."

We crossed the road directly across from Brother Brown's wheel. Next to his last row of trees, water was pouring out of what looked like a hole in the ground. It filled a deep ditch that ran parallel to the road. We followed Brother Brown past ten rows of trees until we came to a tarp that had been set across the ditch and held in place by rocks.

"Got to make a little dam for the water," said Brother Brown, gesturing toward the tarp.

He adjusted the tarp and then waited until the water level had raised to about half the ditch's height.

"You know about siphoning?" he asked, looking at me. He gestured to some aluminum pipes lying on the ground.

My face grimaced and my stomach began to hurt. He didn't expect me to start sucking ditch water through those pipes, did he? "Yes," I said nervously.

"Grab a few of those pipes and get 'em going," he said sharply.

I picked up the nearest pipe and put one end in the ditch. I reluctantly knelt down on the ground and put my lips on the other end, ready to suck.

"No, no, not like that," snapped Brother Brown. He grabbed the pipe from me and shook his head. He put one end in the ditch and covered the other with his hand and then moved the pipe back and forth two times. Water poured out of one end, and he dropped it on the ground so it filled a small ditch dug parallel to one of the rows of trees.

"What did you do? Can you show us again?" I asked, as if begging him to reveal a magic trick.

He grabbed another pipe and moved a little slower this time. "Keep covering the one end while you push it into the ditch. Uncover it when you pull out," he said as he rocked the pipe back and forth. In a few motions, water came spurting out and he laid the pipe on the ground.

"Need three pipes on each side of every row," he said as he moved to grab more pipes.

"Okay, let me give it a try," I said, turning to the others.

I grabbed a pipe and worked frantically to start it siphoning. No matter how fast or how slow I tried, nothing seemed to happen.

"You're not doing your hands right," said Lisa.

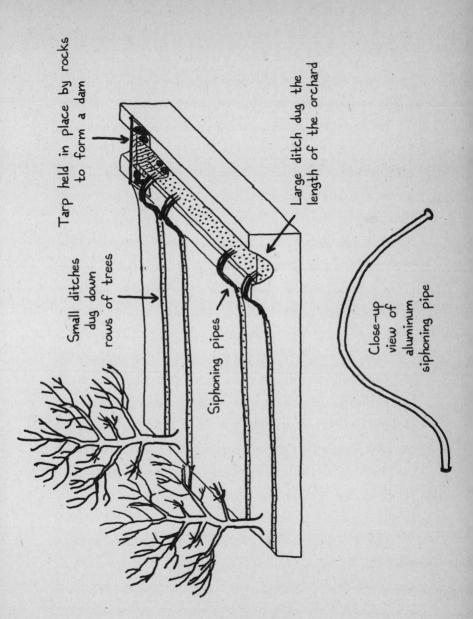

Tarp held in place by rocks to form a dam

Large ditch dug the length of the orchard

Small ditches dug down rows of trees

Siphoning pipes

Close-up view of aluminum siphoning pipe

I looked from face to face. Brother Brown was already a few rows away, leaving us behind. I looked at Amy, who had a calm, uninterested expression.

"Amy, you try, okay?" I pleaded.

She grabbed the pipe and moved me out of the way, positioning herself next to the ditch. She put one hand carefully on the open end of the pipe. With two quick motions, water came bursting out and she dropped the pipe in place. She turned to us with a satisfied smile. Jennifer clapped and yelled, "Yay!" I shook my head.

We all got in line for siphoning lessons from Amy. She proved to be a much more patient teacher than Brother Brown. He finished starting pipes for all the rows and came back to find us all still practicing. Little streams of water were now filling the ditches next to the trees.

Brother Brown grabbed a shovel that was sitting near the tarp dam and headed into the trees. "Gotta check the rows for breaks," he said. We followed along and watched as he moved dirt around in the little ditches to keep water moving along or prevent it from spilling out into the middle of a row. He mostly tried to ignore us.

Finally he said, "I'll let that run a few hours," and he started walking toward his house.

I could sense that the lesson was over but wanted to get some last-minute clarifications. "So this is the same way Mr. Nelson used to do his irrigation?" I asked, following him through the trees.

"Yep, pretty much."

"Where does the water go at the end of all these rows?"

"The runoff goes down another ditch that heads back to the river."

"And how often should I water like this?"

"Oh, about once a week."

There was so much more I wanted to ask him, so many mistakes I was sure we were going to make. We emerged from the trees next to a machine similar to the one I had seen in our orchard with all the small metal wheels. He turned to me and said, "I better be getting inside."

"Thanks a lot, Brother Brown. I uh, uh . . ." I couldn't decide what the most important thing to ask was. I finally said, "Can you tell me what this thing does?" pointing at the mysterious machine.

"Call it a disc. Use it to mix up the soil. Good for weeds too," he said, and continued toward his house.

"Thanks again," I called.

"Thank you," yelled Lisa and Jennifer.

We climbed back on the tractor and wagon for the slow ride home. I noticed that no one's shoes were wet. A little muddy, but dry at the socks. As I leaned over the side of the wagon watching the road, I remembered where I had seen those aluminum siphoning pipes before—Mr. Nelson's old shed.

After school the next day, Amy, Sam, Michael, and I headed across the road to try and find our irrigation gate. We climbed to the top of the embankment, and the boys and I began inching our way toward the trees and plants that grew next to the deep, fast-moving water.

"I don't want to sound bossy, but maybe that isn't the safest thing to do," yelled Amy.

"What should we do, then?" I called back.

"I don't know for sure, but you boys are all pretty clumsy, and I don't want them to have to fish your drowned bodies out of the canal."

We decided it would be safest if only Amy and I got near the water's edge. Sam and Michael were supposed to walk along the top of the canal watching us so they could run for help if Amy or I fell in. The boys didn't like the plan much, but Amy told them they had no choice.

Amy and I made our way carefully along the canal's edge, holding on to the trees and weeds to avoid slipping into the water. After an hour of searching, Amy spotted a rusty wheel hidden in some willows.

"This has to be it!" I shouted. "Sam and Michael, pile a bunch of rocks up on the bank so we can find it again."

We moved aside the trees, and I grabbed the wheel and tried to turn it. It wouldn't budge, even when Amy and I tried turning it together. It took half a can of motor oil and the leverage of a long metal bar to finally get the wheel moving. I gave a cheer as the gate creaked open and water began to swirl around it.

"Guys, go see if it's coming out somewhere across the road," I called. Sam and Michael took off across the road and ducked through the barbed-wire fence that bordered the trees.

By the time I caught up with them, water was pouring out of the ground and spreading over one corner of the orchard. Some was making its way into a ditch like Brother Brown's, but most of it was flooding through the trees, carrying weeds, dirt, and manure with it.

"I don't think it's going where it's supposed to," said Sam, dancing around the spreading water.

"Turn it off! Close the gate!" I shouted to Amy, who was still across the highway.

We stopped the flood and returned to inspect the damage. "We need a better ditch if we want to use those pipes," said Amy. There were still traces of the ditch Mr. Nelson must have used, but after years of neglect, some spots had completely caved in.

"I think this is the type of thing you need a plow for," I said while moving some of the dirt around.

"Why don't we hook that plow in the middle of the orchard up to the tractor?" suggested Sam, always eager to use the tractor.

When we went to look at the plow, I shook my head

doubtfully. "I'm not sure how you'd connect it to the tractor. And it's so heavy, I don't think we could move it into place, anyway," I said, kicking it.

"We'll have to get our dads to help again. Jackson, go get your dad and I'll get mine. I'll pull the tractor over by this thing, and we'll meet you back here," said Amy decisively.

Our dads moaned and complained but followed the tractor out to the plow. They circled around it a few times, talking with each other about how it might attach. My dad then backed the tractor up to it, and Uncle David and the rest of us pushed against the plow until some of its arms seemed to match the holes and rings on the back of the tractor. My uncle slid some pins in place and stepped back.

"I can't believe that fits! What are the odds?" yelled my uncle. He and my dad were mostly used to parts not matching up.

They were actually excited to drive the tractor around with the plow on it for a few minutes. They figured out which of the tractor's levers to push to make the plow go up and down, and they started digging a little trench down the middle of a row.

"Hey, not there!" Amy shouted.

They finally gave the tractor back, and Amy turned it toward the top of the orchard where the main ditch was supposed to be. We dragged Lisa and Jennifer away from

their homework, and everyone but Amy stood on the plow to weigh it down so we could make the deepest cut possible into the ground. Someone fell off every few feet and had to run and jump back on as Amy steadily drove the length of the orchard. After three passes, we decided the new ditch wasn't getting any deeper and would have to be good enough.

⸻

The next day we gave watering another try and pulled all the aluminum pipes from Mr. Nelson's tool shed. Underneath the pipes, we found the tarps for making the little dam and secured them in the ditch with some rocks.

"Okay, Amy, you go turn on the water. I'm going to grab every shovel I can find. I have a feeling we'll be needing them," I said to her.

"Everyone else stay here and stay out of the ditch," Amy warned, looking at Sam and Michael.

When I got back with the shovels, water was already pouring out of the ground and most of it was running down the new ditch. Sam and I frantically shoveled dirt and mud to redirect any water moving in the wrong direction. When we reached the dam and tarp, lots of water was leaking around it, but Amy and my sisters were starting siphoning pipes, anyway.

"See what you can do about the dam," Amy demanded.

We got the dam more secure, but the ditch just wasn't very deep and the pipes were hard to start. After a lot of complaining, though, Amy had water dribbling out toward the first ten rows of trees.

"I'll stay here and watch the pipes with the girls," Amy said to me. "You take the boys and figure out where the water's going." She smiled, thinking most of her work was done.

Looking down the rows of trees, it was easy to see there were no nice ditches to channel the water like in Brother Brown's orchard. There may have been at one time, but they were now long gone. Instead, the flowing water was making its own little paths, cutting across some rows and filling the middle of others. Manure and weeds were carried down the rows, blocking off some of the water's escape.

Sam, Michael, and I tried to unblock some of the largest obstacles to help even out the water flow. We also shoveled to try and redirect water, but as fast as we fixed breaks, new ones appeared. Water eventually reached the end of some of the rows. There was nothing to catch it, so it flowed right toward our houses. It formed large puddles in the driveway and pooled up in our yards.

My dad came running into the orchard. "You bird-brains better turn off that water or you're going to flood this whole place!"

I ran back toward Amy, waving my arms. "Turn it off! Turn it off! It's going everywhere!" I screamed.

Amy and the girls were sitting by the ditch, laughing together, but Amy jumped up and ran across the road to the gate. We spent the rest of the day driving the tractor back and forth through the orchard making little ditches down every row.

The yards of our houses had dried out by Sunday afternoon. By then, my mom and aunt decided they would like the yards to be flooded periodically so they could have a real lawn and flower garden. Amy told them they would probably get it whether they liked it or not.

————

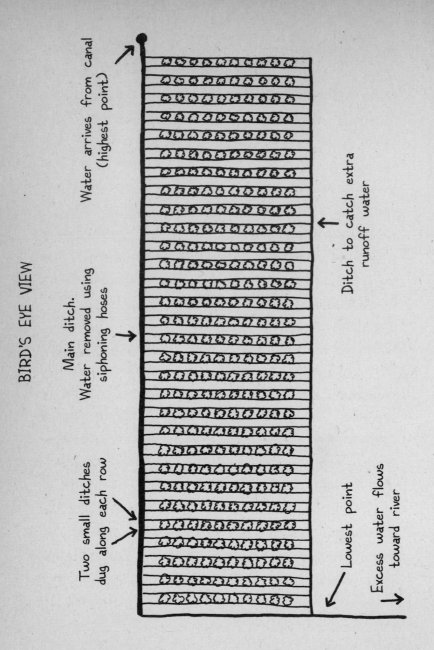

BIRD'S EYE VIEW

Water arrives from canal (highest point)

Main ditch.
Water removed using siphoning hoses

Two small ditches dug along each row

Ditch to catch extra runoff water

Lowest point
Excess water flows toward river

On Monday after school, we cranked the water on again. The ditch filled up to the dam, and we let Amy start all the pipes while Sam, Michael, and I watched the rows. There were little breaks, but nothing like what happened on Saturday. We dug and filled to get the channels just right, and soon ten rows had shining streams of water flowing toward them. We left the water running until it was dark and then crossed over the road holding flashlights and turned off the gate. On Tuesday we moved the dams and pipes and repeated the process on the next ten rows. On Wednesday we did the same thing for the last ten.

Amy was never really happy with our first main ditch, and Sam, Michael, and I were forced to dig it deeper with shovels for the next two months. Our hands became thick with calluses, and as we dug we would refer to Amy as "the ditch witch."

After a few rounds, watering became pretty routine and floods a rarity. Eventually, I was as good at starting the siphon hoses as Amy, although she would never admit it. We even dug a couple of shallow trenches into our yards and would flood my mom's lawn once a week. She said it never looked greener, and my dad said it had never looked cheaper. Sometimes we would take off our shoes and walk around barefoot in the water splashing each other. Almost like we were kids.

Chapter 10
POISON SHOWERS

I was feeling pretty confident after our first success-
ful round of watering. I had even stomped up to Mrs.
Nelson's door with muddy shoes to show her the little
beginnings of apples on a branch I had pulled off.

"I think we figured it out," I said, telling her about the
watering. "Just a matter of time now for these apples."

"That's nice," she said, looking at the branch. There
was none of the enthusiasm she had showed toward the
blossoms.

My parents were equally ambivalent. They didn't seem
to realize how incredible it was for a bunch of kids to

figure out irrigation, no matter how difficult I made it sound. The one adult I hoped might appreciate our success was Brother Brown. I cornered him after Sunday school again.

"We got those trees watered after all," I said. "Even figured out our plow." I had a proud grin on my face and was hoping to hear some congratulations.

Brother Brown looked me up and down. "You get those trees sprayed yet?" he croaked out.

My face fell. "Sprayed with what?"

"Somethin' to kill the worms."

"What worms?" I paused to think if I had read about worms. "Are they really that bad? Do you have to kill 'em?" I asked, my voice getting higher as I spoke.

"Not if you like sharin' your apples with 'em."

It was one unpleasant surprise after another with these apples. "What am I supposed to do about it? Can I watch you do some spraying?" I asked.

"Nah. Go down to General Supply. Tell 'em you want something for worms."

"But then what?"

"They'll help you. And you're smart."

He walked off with all my confidence. Back home I looked over the pages I had copied from the apple book. There were a few things about bugs and larva, but I hadn't written anything too specific. I began to remember, though, that the book had talked about natural and chemical ways to kill bugs. At the time I had tried to ignore that part, hoping it was something I wouldn't have to deal with. Bugs seemed like a bigger problem for people living in swamps than on New Mexican plateaus.

I remembered, too, that natural bug control sounded good to me. The book had talked about using ladybugs and things like that. How could I be sure, though, that the Haslam guy who wrote it had ever raised his own apples? The only person I knew who had was Brother Brown. And if he used something from General Supply, that was probably the way to go. Getting fancy with ladybugs might be risky.

I explained to my cousins that we needed to make a trip to investigate worm spraying.

"Let me guess how you think we're getting there," said Amy with a frown. "If it's on the tractor, I'm not going. You can take one of these two with you. They don't have a reputation to worry about."

I would definitely have preferred her. "So who wants to go with me?" I asked the boys.

"Me!" they both said in unison.

That started an argument about why I didn't want to keep track of them both. A coin flip followed, along with a promise to the loser that they would get to go the next time.

Between our house and Farmington was Fruitland.

Fruitland wasn't really a town by any strict definitions. It was mostly just a name. There was no mayor or police or city limits, just some houses and a post office. Maybe our house was even part of Fruitland. Everyone I knew drove into Farmington if they wanted to shop for food or clothes or toothpaste because the only store in Fruitland was General Supply. I hadn't been there much, mostly for emergencies, like when we ran out of toilet paper.

A tractor going down the side of the road in Fruitland was pretty common, so no one paid much attention to Sam and me on our way to General Supply. Even in third gear and full throttle, it took us about twenty minutes to get there. I parked the tractor out front on the torn-up pavement next to some beaten-up pickup trucks.

When you walked into General Supply, you had to give your eyes a few seconds to adjust to all the shapes and colors. Every inch of the place from floor to ceiling held something for sale. A bell over the door rang as Sam and I moved inside. We quickly shuffled toward a dimly lit back section and began to look around.

We kept moving until we saw saddles and harnesses and then salt licks and different bags of feed. "This looks kind of like a farming section," I whispered to Sam. "I'll bet what we're looking for is around here somewhere."

Sam wasn't paying attention because he was poking at the baby chicks for sale in a big wire pen.

I walked up and down looking at various "chows" for dogs and rabbits and sheep. There were bags full of baby goat formula but nothing that looked like worm poison.

"Maybe we should ask someone," said Sam, who was following me.

I looked around nervously. "But I don't know anyone. They might think we're idiots," I whispered. I wished Amy had come.

After another few minutes of random searching, I had to agree with Sam. We moved back toward the front of the store and hid behind some shelves so I could spy on whoever worked there.

The store seemed to have two employees. One was a huge man who looked tall even though he was sitting on a stool behind a counter. He was talking loudly with a customer, and his big stomach would shake against the counter as he laughed.

The other worker looked like he was in high school, maybe three or four years older than me, although I didn't recognize him. He was trying to add up someone's purchases and kept looking nervously at the huge man and brushing his messy hair out of his face. I waited until he was done with his customer and then hurried up to him.

"Hi," I began.

"Can I help you?" he asked, looking unsure of himself.

"Do you know anything about sprays? Worm poisons you could use on apple trees?"

"Well, I don't really know too much about them." He looked over at the fat man. "I could probably show you where they are, though."

I don't know why I liked him, but I did. Maybe it was because he was more flustered and nervous than I was. Sam and I followed him toward the back of the store near the baby chicks.

"So how long have you been working here?" I asked, trying to sound friendly.

"About three weeks. After school and Saturdays. I still don't know my way around very well."

"I'm Jackson and this is Sam."

"I'm Jimmy. So here's where most of this stuff is. Do you know what kind you need?" He pointed at a group of dusty bags on one of the shelves.

"No, not really," I said, staring at them. "Do you know what kind Jess Brown uses?"

"Jess Brown?"

"He's kind of short. Wears blue bib overalls. Talks in a croaky voice."

A look of recognition crossed over Jimmy's face. "Oh yeah. He was in here a couple of days ago and bought a bunch of this, uh . . ."—he pointed his finger along a few of the bags—"Diazinon."

"That's what we need, then."

Jimmy grabbed one of the bags and started walking back toward the front. We followed him wordlessly.

"So will that be cash or charge?" asked Jimmy, setting the bag on the glass counter.

I hadn't thought about the fact that bug spray would cost money. I guess just finding out about the spray seemed like such a huge obstacle, I never bothered thinking about what came next.

Since I didn't have any money, I said, "Maybe I could charge it."

"Do you have an account set up already? Or maybe your parents?" Jimmy looked hopefully at me, trying his best to be helpful.

"Can you check for my dad's account? Dan Jones?"

Jimmy turned around and grabbed what looked like an old shoebox. Inside was a collection of cards with names and numbers on them. He thumbed through looking for Dan Jones while Sam and I waited nervously.

"Ah, here it is," he said, pulling the card out. "Hasn't had anything charged in a long time," he said, inspecting it. "Shall I put the Diazinon down?"

I turned to look at Sam, but he quickly turned away, trying to avoid any involvement in what I was about to do.

"How much is it?" I asked Jimmy weakly.

"Twenty dollars."

"Yeah, I guess you better put it down," I said slowly. "How often are you supposed to come in and pay that, anyway?"

"I don't know," said Jimmy starting to write. "From the looks of some of these cards, not very often."

That cheered me up a little.

"Do you have any tools that you could use to do the actual spraying?" I asked Jimmy, looking at the bag. "'Cause this is like a powder that I would pour into water and mix up, right?"

"I know we have some hand sprayers I can show you."

He led me to where a couple of the hand sprayers were sitting on a shelf. They looked to hold about two gallons of water and had a handle that you could pump to pressurize the liquid inside. There was also a little nozzle attached to a hose.

"I think people mostly use these to spray around their houses, to kill ants and things like that," Jimmy said, demonstrating how the pump worked. He let me try too.

"How many trees do you have to spray?" he asked.

"Three hundred."

"Oh, man, it'd probably take a year with one of those," he said, shaking his head. "I think most people doing that kind of job have big tanks and pumps."

I looked around the store feeling discouraged. "I guess I'll have to figure something else out," I finally said.

As we walked back toward the front, we passed the cold case holding the cans of pop. Sam motioned toward it and gave me a begging look.

"Better get one for Amy and Michael too," I said to him.

"Can we charge these four pops too?" I asked Jimmy when we got to the counter. "Oh, and we might as well fill up the tractor with gas."

"Anything else?" he asked as he wrote on the card.

I looked at the bag of poison again. "Any idea how much water to mix up with it?"

Jimmy turned to the fat man sitting on the stool.

"Mr. Sherwood, how much water should you mix with this stuff?" he called out, holding up the bag.

"One bag to about two hundred gallons," the man yelled back very loudly, eyeing me closely.

"How much should you put on a tree?" I asked Jimmy.

"How much should you put on a tree?" he called out to the man again.

"About half a gallon."

"Should be good for about four hundred trees, then," said Jimmy.

We filled up the tractor with Jimmy's help at the old gas pump outside.

"Thanks a lot," I shouted to him as we drove off with Sam sitting in the wagon to make sure the Diazinon and pops didn't fall out. "We'll be seeing you again."

I placed my hopes in there being something in Mr. Nelson's old shed that could be used for spraying. My cousins and I had taken quite a few things out of the shed already, but there were still lots of cardboard boxes and bags around and various mechanical parts scattered everywhere. I rummaged through them, not really sure what a pump would look like. My eyes kept coming back to a coil of black tubing that looked like a long garden hose. I grabbed the tubing and started to unravel it. At one end was a metal gun shaped just like a big water pistol. It had a trigger and everything. I pulled the whole contraption out of the shed to investigate.

The other end of the hose was attached to a round metal piece with a hole in the middle that then led to a long straight pipe. I laid the hose out in the driveway next to my house and tried to figure out how the thing worked. The round piece had a section that turned around inside. If it was a pump, it was hard to see how a person was supposed to turn it.

My dad arrived home from work as I was playing with the round, turning piece. He pulled up beside me and jumped out of his car.

"What's this?" he asked with an interested look on his face.

"I'm not sure. I think it could be some kind of pump and water sprayer."

He looked it over. "Where'd you get it?"

"Mr. Nelson's shed."

I could tell he was curious because he was already grabbing the gun and pulling the trigger. I knew that if I could just keep him interested, he might be able to figure it out.

"I think this part is a pump, if I only knew how it worked." I pointed toward the round piece. "I'll bet this thing can really shoot out lots of water!"

He moved over and started spinning the inner piece I had showed him. "Hmm ... uh-huh," he grunted. "Looks like you attach this to some sort of shaft that turns this around ..." he mumbled to himself. He turned the piece over in his hands for a minute and then stopped. He looked up and squinted his eyes. "I wonder if that ..."

All of a sudden, he got up and walked toward the other side of the house carrying the piece with him. "Drag those hoses over here," he called to me.

We pulled everything to the tractor, and he knelt behind its rear axle where we would usually attach the plow or wagon. He lifted up the round piece and slid it over a metal shaft that stuck out of the tractor.

"Well, that is two for two for this thing. I can't believe it fits," he said, staring in awe at the piece. "See, I think that shaft spins around on the tractor powering the pump."

"Wow, how did you figure that out?" I asked, sincerely impressed.

"When we were messing around with that plow, I noticed how one of those levers would make the shaft turn but I wasn't sure why. I guess it's to run things like this." He looked very pleased with himself. "Shall we try it?"

"Sure!" I shouted.

We grabbed a five-gallon bucket from inside the house and filled it with water. We figured we were supposed to put the long straight tube into the water source, so we stuck it in the bucket. Dad turned on the tractor and started the shaft spinning. He ran back to the gun and pulled the trigger. Nothing happened.

"I bet we have to prime it!" he yelled.

He pulled the straight pipe out of the bucket and poured water into it. "Go pull the trigger!" he called to me. When I did, a stream of water shot out. He lowered the pipe into the bucket and called for the gun. After a few shots of water into the air, he said, "Go get your mother," with an evil grin on his face.

I started for the door, but he chickened out and instead shot the rest of the bucket's load onto the side of the house. He turned off the tractor, still admiring his work.

"So how much water do you think this thing can pump?" I asked him.

"A lot. It sucked out that bucket like crazy."

"What if I had to pump out a lot more than just a few gallons?"

"Get a bigger bucket, then. What are you trying to pump?"

"I've got to spray all the trees with something to keep the worms from eating the apples. And it takes a lot of the stuff."

He thought for a few seconds. "You know the cheapest thing to do would be to get an empty fifty-five gallon oil drum. Looking at the length of that straight pipe, I'll bet that's what Jack Nelson did."

"How could I get one? Where do you find 'em?"

He was quiet while he debated with himself as to whether he should get more involved. Eventually, the part of him that wanted to see a fifty-five-gallon water gun won out.

"There's a few of them behind the bolt store. I'll try to bring one home tomorrow if I can figure out a way to attach it to the car."

"Thanks, Dad! It's great to have someone who can build and fix things."

"Yeah, yeah." He ignored my attempted compliment and went into the house.

———————⇥

I helped with the irrigation on the following day until I heard my dad drive up. "Gotta go!" I said, and handed my shovel to Amy.

There was a barrel tied awkwardly to the open trunk

162

of the Dodge Dart my dad was driving. He was untying it and looking very grumpy.

"Wow, you got it!" I said excitedly.

"Barely," he replied in disgust. "One side came untied on the way home. The stupid thing started dragging down the road, sparks flying everywhere. I'm lucky it didn't kill someone."

I could see the deep scratches on one end of the barrel. Once untied, we rolled it over to the wagon and lifted it up. My dad used some wire to wrap around the barrel and the sides of the wagon to hold it in place.

"There you go. There's your barrel," he said, and then started walking away.

"Aren't you going to stay and see it working?" I yelled to him.

"The less I see of that, that"—I could tell he was trying not to swear—"that dadgum barrel, the better," he finally spit out.

"Thank you!" I yelled before he disappeared inside our house.

I attached the wagon to the tractor and pushed the long pipe that connected to the pump into the opening in the barrel. My dad was right—it fit almost perfectly. I grabbed the hose and filled the barrel to the top, hoping my dad didn't notice me using city water.

I wanted to surprise my sisters and cousins, so I drove

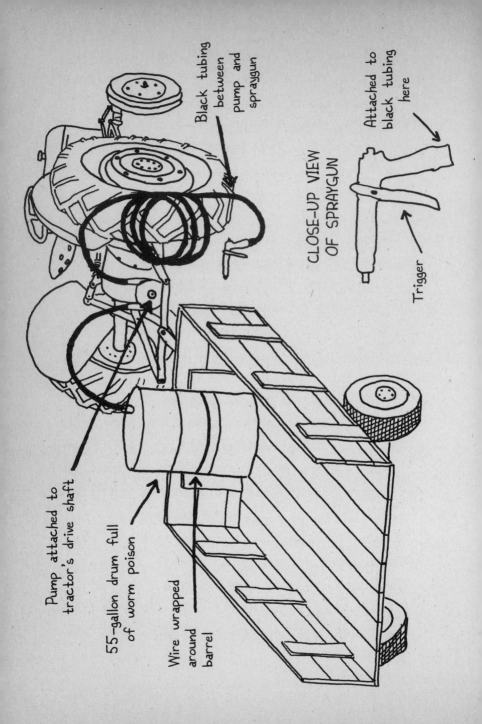

Black tubing between pump and spraygun

CLOSE-UP VIEW OF SPRAYGUN

Attached to black tubing here

Trigger

Pump attached to tractor's drive shaft

55-gallon drum full of worm poison

Wire wrapped around barrel

the tractor out into the orchard. "Wait till you see what this can do," I said, pointing toward the barrel and spray gun.

I grabbed the gun and flipped the lever to turn on the pump. I squeezed the trigger. Nothing happened.

"Impressive," said Lisa, giggling.

"Hold on!" I said, and ran back to the house for a jug of water.

"You've got to prime it!" I yelled as I poured the water into the straight pipe that led to the pump. I put the pipe back in the barrel, flipped the lever, and pulled the trigger. I had the gun pointing at the girls, and they scattered as a jet of water came shooting out.

"Cool!" shouted Sam and Michael. "Let me try!" they yelled together.

We all got a chance to hold the gun and try to spray each other. The gun's nozzle adjusted so it could shoot a stream of water over fifty feet, and there weren't many places to hide. Eventually, we were all standing around the tractor shivering. It was the kind of thing you wished you were doing in July instead of late April.

"So who wants to help me spray tomorrow?" I asked.

"I will!" said Sam and Michael.

"Is it dangerous for people?" Lisa asked.

"I don't think it can be that good for you," I admitted. We all looked around at each other. "You better do it.

Sam can drive the tractor," Amy said. "And wear those handkerchiefs you used to wear for the manure."

I felt a little nervous as I drove the tractor back toward our house to top off the barrel with water. How dangerous could it be? Brother Brown was still alive, and he must have been doing it for fifty years. For all I knew, though, he was twenty and the poison was just making him look old. Maybe it was affecting his voice too.

———⌐

Sam and I opened the bag of Diazinon the next afternoon. We wore handkerchiefs over our noses and mouths, but the powder inside still had a sickly chemical smell. I poured a quarter of the bag into the barrel and then tried stirring it with a stick.

"This isn't working so well, but I've got an idea," I said, and jammed the spray gun into the barrel's opening. I turned on the pump, and the water in the barrel swirled into a bubbly froth. After five minutes I said, "That's gotta do it."

After following Sam and the tractor out to the orchard, I adjusted the nozzle and took aim at the first tree, directing the stream of water up and down. I had no idea how much to apply, so I just tried to cover all the leaves and branches. Spraying the first row was kind of fun, but then I began to smell the poison through my handkerchief and feel a fine mist of it settle over me.

The gun quickly became so heavy that I had to prop it against my body for support.

The barrel was dry by the end of eight rows and the stream of poison stopped. My head was throbbing sharply, and I felt sick to my stomach. I threw the hose and gun into the wagon and climbed in for the ride home.

Sam looked wet from the poison mist when he climbed off the tractor.

"How do you feel?" I asked. "You all right?"

"Kind of have a headache and a little stomachache."

"I'm going to go in and take a shower and get everything cleaned off me. You should too."

The warm shower made me feel better, but I still felt like I couldn't quite get everything off my skin. I barely ate any dinner and crawled into bed afraid I would wake up a mutant.

On the way home from school the next day, I didn't say anything to Sam about more spraying. Walking past the orchard brought back the sick feeling, and I headed straight for my bedroom and shut the door. Breathing in that poison had to be bad for us. Maybe enough of it would even kill us. I didn't want to see that barrel or gun again, and I thought up ways to avoid them.

The only sure way was abandoning the whole project. I quickly thought up more reasons to justify walking away. For instance, Brother Brown was bound to have more miserable apple-growing surprises waiting for me even if I could get past spraying.

I pulled the contract out of my encyclopedia and read it over: $8,000. How was that going to be possible? I was killing myself for nothing! Continuing was just going to make it worse and make everyone hate me more when they didn't get any money. Yes. It was best for everyone just to stop now.

There was a knock on my door, and when I answered it, Sam was standing there. "You ready to go?" he asked. He already had his handkerchief around his face.

His eyes stopped me from telling him it was all useless and dangerous. They expected something. I didn't want them looking at me like I was a quitter.

"Yeah, but let's move faster on the next run."

The next two days brought the same pain. I stopped being quite as careful, and we finished spraying the remaining twenty-two rows using only two more barrels worth of poison.

"So that's it, right?" asked Sam after we parked the tractor.

"You mean for today or forever?"

"I was hoping forever."

"Me, too, but I'll have to find out from someone how many times we're supposed to do this."

I thought I would throw up when Brother Brown

told me we should spray every other week. Those lady-bugs had to be a better idea. Sam and I experimented with different face coverings to keep out as much spray as possible. The best facemasks were the little white ones painters wore. We found them stuffed into a forgotten corner at General Supply.

We also decided it was better to get the misery over all at once, so we started spraying the whole orchard in a single day—three barrels, one right after another. During spray days, I couldn't remember why Slim's scrap yard had seemed so bad.

Chapter 11
SUMMER VACATION

School got out for the summer in late May. Classes ended on a Thursday, which didn't make much sense to me. The junior high had a big dance every year on the last day of school as a type of celebration. This was especially important for the ninth graders like Amy who would be moving on to high school the next year. It was their last chance for a while to feel big and important. Amy had been talking about it for months and had arranged to go with some of her friends.

"So, are you coming?" she asked me a couple of weeks before. "You can probably ride with me."

"I dunno," I told Amy reluctantly. "I don't really know how to dance."

"Oh, that doesn't matter," she said. "No one does. You just kind of move to the music."

"That's easy for you to say. You're probably good at it."

"Come on, it's fun. You're not still afraid of girls, are you?" she teased.

"No! I just don't wanna embarrass myself."

"What if I show you some moves and you could practice a little?"

"Maybe," I said, feeling a little less anxious.

That night I went to Amy's room to practice. She had recorded some of her favorite songs from the radio using her cassette player, and she started playing the tape. She tried to demonstrate how you should move back and forth and use both your feet and your arms. She looked pretty natural doing it, like she wasn't even thinking.

When I tried, she gave me a doubtful look. "You'll get it. You should just practice more by yourself. Your feet look like they're barely moving. Don't look so stiff and scared."

I promised to practice more. Amy explained that there weren't really many slow songs played at these dances but that we should probably go over slow dancing just in case. She showed me where to put my arms, and we moved around her room to "We've Got Tonight" by Kenny Rogers and Sheena Easton. "Just stay on the

171

beat," Amy insisted. "Take it nice and slow, and don't get all panicky."

The song ended and Aunt Sandy was standing in the doorway, trying not to laugh. "You two do know you're cousins, right?" she asked with a wide grin.

I practiced a little every night in my room, not daring to let anyone see me. The night of the dance, I ironed my best long-sleeve shirt and church pants and sprinkled some of my dad's English Leather cologne on my neck.

The mom of one of Amy's friends came and picked us up. Four of us piled into the back of her huge Olds Cutlass. Amy had on what she considered her best clothes and even a little makeup. The whole ride to school was a blur because I was so nervous. I mostly kept my mouth shut and hugged one of the doors.

The junior high cafeteria had been transformed into a dance hall by hanging up lengths of crepe paper around all the doors, setting up a table littered with paper cups full of punch, and turning off most of the lights. The effort had taken dozens of teenagers months to plan and execute.

Music was already playing when we arrived, and kids were milling around in various groups with a few people dancing in the middle of the room. Amy was quickly swallowed up by her ninth-grade friends and soon afterward had pushed a large number of them into the dancing area.

I looked around desperately for familiar faces and saw Chantz Eyring and Jimmy Bradshaw near the punch table. I had never had much to do with them before, but it was amazing how much you could find to talk about when you were pretending to not be interested in dancing. It was also amazing how many tiny sips of punch you could get out of one cup when you were looking for something to do with your hands.

Just when I thought I might get away with not dancing at all, Amy sent her friend Paige Manning over. "Would you like to dance?" asked Paige playfully.

"Sure," I said, and followed her toward the middle of the room. My heart rate accelerated, and I tried to remember everything Amy had taught me. "Come on Eileen" was blaring from the speakers, and I did my best to move my arms and legs. I hardly dared look at Paige and mostly kept my head down. I caught a glimpse of Amy, and she mouthed to me, "Smile!" I faked a grin and held out to the end. I thanked Paige and fled back to a corner, hoping no one was watching too carefully.

Half an hour later, Amy sent over Stacy Tanner to repeat the experience. This time we got "Little Red Corvette" by Prince. I looked up more, and Stacy kept smiling back at me encouragingly.

Amy left me alone after that, and I was able to shrink into the shadows and just watch. I mostly watched her. She moved effortlessly around the room, dancing and talking to everyone. She looked genuinely happy and not the least bit self-conscious. She seemed so much older than me. I felt a wave of guilt for convincing her to help me with the orchard. Weeds and mud and dead apple branches all seemed so beneath her.

The dance ended at ten, and I got dropped off at home before Amy and her friends drove off somewhere together.

———————⟩

I woke up on Friday morning at the time I usually would on a school day but lay in bed staring up at my ceiling. If a car had driven by dropping Amy off, I had slept through it, so I wondered when she made it home. I decided I deserved to sleep in a little, but right before I could fall back to sleep, my sisters barged into my room.

"Wake up, lazy," said Lisa derisively. She and Jennifer started bouncing on my bed.

"What do you want? Go away!" I grunted, and tried to roll over.

"Is this what you're going to do all summer? You think we're going to do all the work while you lay around?" Lisa teased.

"What are you talking about?"

"The orchard, dummy. Aren't you supposed to be in charge? We're not sure what to do."

Somehow it was strange that my sisters cared what

happened to the orchard. I had always thought of it as my project with them only grudgingly involved. I suddenly realized they looked at it as more than that.

"All right! Just give me a minute," I finally said. I slipped on some clothes and found the girls outside waiting for me near the tractor. A few seconds after I got there, Sam and Michael walked out of their house and joined us. It was almost as if they were headed for school, except they weren't carrying any books or bags. We had worked every day except Sundays since we had started in February, but it was still a strange scene.

When Sam and Michael reached us, we all looked around at each other until all four faces were looking at me expectantly. Sam was the first to break the silence.

"So what else needs to be done from here on out?"

It was a little overwhelming to think that they had put so much trust in me. His question caught me off-guard, and I struggled to sound like I knew what I was talking about. I thought back to the calendar I had created. There had been a big gap while waiting for apples to grow, but I didn't dare tell my workforce that and risk destroying our momentum. "Well, uh, we've got to keep up with the spraying and watering. We've also got the rest of those weeds to chop and that ditch to keep digging. Probably best to get the weeds out of the way first. You guys really ready to work all the time now?"

"Why wouldn't we be? I thought that was the idea," said Sam.

"Are we going to get pops every day now that we're working the whole day?" asked Michael.

"Umm, yeah," I replied, trying to think where all those cans were going to come from.

"Where's Amy?" Lisa asked Sam and Michael.

"Probably asleep," said Michael. "Mom was pretty mad this morning about how late she came back home."

Almost half of the rows still needed weeding, so we went to work with our normal method using the shovel, weed whackers, and hoes. My thinking about the weeds was that if they could steal water and nutrients from the trees, they had to go. Having them gone also made the orchard look a lot better and kept everyone busy. I watched carefully as everyone attacked weeds enthusiastically, wondering if they could keep it up all day, every day. And what was all this work really worth in dollars? How many thousands would we have to bring in so they got their fair share?

We didn't see Amy until after lunch. She came walking out to the orchard without any shoes on, still in her pajamas. She looked at us and the freshly cut weeds through tired eyes.

"Hey," she said to me.

"Hi," I responded, avoiding eye contact.

"How was the dance?" asked Lisa.

"It was fun. Really good music," Amy said while trying to shade her eyes from the sun.

"What time did you get home last night?" Michael asked.

"None of your business!" Amy snapped, looking at him angrily.

She kept staring at us and the weeds while we continued working.

"How long have you been out here?" she finally asked.

"Since this morning," Sam answered. "We're full-time now."

I watched her carefully, unsure how she would react. She glared at Sam, who was looking away to avoid her eyes. She shook her head and I thought she was going to walk away, but instead she grabbed the free hoe leaning against a nearby tree. She attacked the closest weeds vigorously in her pajamas and bare feet.

———————

With everyone working full-time, it was amazing how much we could get done. Even with the watering and digging on the ditch, we were on a pace to finish all the weeding by early June. Just a month earlier, there didn't seem to be enough hours in the day. Once the weeds were cut, it didn't seem like there would be enough work to keep six people busy.

The trees themselves looked great, with lots of leaves and little apples on almost every branch. Still, it seemed too good to be true. Were we missing something? I went through my copied apple book pages again. After reading what I had written down for the fourth or fifth time, I was pretty disgusted with my earlier effort. I should have drawn pictures. Nothing seemed to make sense now that the book itself was so far away in my memory. And since summer break had started, there was no chance to check it out again.

I found a few words I had written about apple sizes and not letting them grow too densely. I examined how our apples were growing. Three or four always seemed to be next to each other on adjoining stems. Was this too dense? I thought of trying to get Brother Brown to stop by and take a look. I decided that would be very unlikely, so I did the next best thing.

That Sunday I carried a brown paper grocery bag into our Sunday school class and stuffed it under my chair. Brother Brown eyed the sack suspiciously but didn't ask any questions. After class he waited for me, knowing I wanted to show him something.

"So what have you got?" he asked before I could open the bag.

I pulled out an apple branch I had bent to fit inside. Leaves scattered all over the floor. Brother Brown's eyes flashed with curiosity.

"Can you take a look at this and tell me what you think of the little apples?" I asked.

He grabbed the branch and handled the leaves and little shoots carefully. He held each part up close to his eyes. I held my breath during the examination. Finally he turned to me and spoke.

"Leaves look good. No disease. Lots of apples on here."

I grabbed the branch back eagerly. "So is that good?"

"Good if you like little apples."

"So they're too dense?"

"That's a good word for it. Better pull off two out of every three. Like right here you should just leave one." He pulled off two little apples from a group of three to show me.

"What if I don't pull them off?"

"Then they'll all be small. No one wants to buy a small apple, believe me."

I did believe him, but it seemed like a waste of a lot of good potential apples.

"Brother Brown, is there anything else I need to do? You know, until they're ready to pick?"

"You're sprayin' and waterin'? Keep it up and get 'em thinned out." He paused and added, "Summer's the easy part. Better rest up for what's comin'." His voice didn't sound as harsh as usual.

———————

It was hard to convince my sisters and cousins about apple density. I took them out to a tree and repeated what Brother Brown had said.

179

"It just doesn't sound right," said Lisa. "Don't we want more apples, not less?"

"How do we know he's not tricking you into wasting all our apples?" asked Michael, acting like he had uncovered a conspiracy.

"He is kind of like our competition," said Amy.

"No, no, he wouldn't do something like that. Remember how he showed us how to water," I said, defending Brother Brown.

"And how do we know we're doing that right?" asked Michael.

"Well, it seems to be working so far. Look, I think the reason we have to do it is the same reason we did the pruning. We want the tree to concentrate its energy on growing fewer apples a lot bigger. Do you like eating small apples?"

"How small?" asked Michael.

At that point, I turned to Amy for help.

"I guess it makes sense," she finally said, and the others eventually went along.

Thinning reminded me a lot of pruning and, I imagined, what picking must be like. We had to use the ladders to reach every group of apples. Sam climbed all through the inside of each tree pulling off two little apples for each one he left. We sent Michael in there with him and assigned Lisa and Jennifer to the lowest-hanging branches.

I wasn't exactly sure what kept them coming back day after day. Michael always talked about the money he was going to make and the cans of pop. Sam just seemed happy to be outside and doing what everyone else was. My sisters had a competitiveness that wouldn't let them sit around while we were working. Besides all those things, though, I think they all had become a little attached to the trees. They would look at the tiny apples they were pulling off and say, "Do you really think these are going to be the size of regular apples someday?" Watching air and water turn into something they could hold and eat was like learning an ancient magic they wanted to be a part of.

My favorite times were when Amy and I were working by ourselves on a tree. I would mostly just listen to her ramble. She loved to tell me about all the people at school and who liked whom. I knew most of them only through Amy's stories, but I still liked the way she took all of their lives so seriously. She seemed to have no interest in the future beyond her next three years of high school. I tried to get her to tell me what she was going to do after that, but she would always change the subject. Even when we played our favorite game, "would you rather," she limited her opinions to things in the short term. When I asked, "Would you rather live in a trailer but drive a Ferrari or live in a mansion but drive a VW Bug?" she didn't seem to care. But when I asked about

Homecoming queen versus Prom queen, her opinions were very strong about Homecoming queen. I didn't understand it much and decided it must have something to do with being a girl.

It was amazing to see what we could accomplish working full-time. The thinning was done in only three weeks, and by the time July hit, there wasn't much for six people to do, really. The weeds in the orchard had completely surrendered and been wiped out. Sam even became obsessed with pulling the discing machine behind the tractor to churn and chop up weeds we'd missed.

Every other week I would take the tractor to General Supply and buy more Diazinon and cans of pop for full workdays. I probably could have bought enough for the whole summer in one trip, but I kind of liked driving to the store. In the furniture section, there was a huge air conditioner. It felt great on a hot day to sit on the couches and chairs and be drenched by the cool air and then wander around the store examining all the strange things for sale. When Michael figured out their charge system, he begged me to buy him all kinds of things, especially a BB gun and a baby chick.

Eventually, the girls only joined us on watering days. The hotter it got, the more we all looked forward to irrigating and would do it without shoes on and in rolled-up pants. Sitting underneath the shade of the trees with the water rolling over our feet was the coolest place we had.

The one activity we never seemed to finish was digging out the ditches by hand. With the hot July sun beating down, we didn't work very hard at that, though. Ditch digging was usually relegated to Sam, Michael, and me. If we did nothing else on a particular day, I always made sure we moved our shovels around a little. When my dad would ask me at night what I'd done during the day, I could always at least answer, "Dug a ditch." He would reply that was better than nothing but that I would be better off down at the scrap yard.

———⌐

The deeper we got into the summer, the less I talked with or even saw Mrs. Nelson. Right after school let out, when we were thinning or weeding, she would occasionally watch from her window and walk out to talk sometimes as I passed by her house. As the temperatures rose, she stopped coming out as much. Finally, she stayed inside altogether. I took her branches and samples of the apples every few weeks so she could see how well they were growing. The bigger the apples got, the less interested she seemed. Sometimes she would even pretend not to be home, but I would leave my samples by the front door, anyway. The way she acted worried me more and more.

I had reread our contract enough times to memorize it during the first weeks of pruning. Since then I had mostly left it in its hiding place, almost afraid to think about it. I had pushed it into some future place in my head. Maybe Mrs. Nelson had too. But after five months of work, I couldn't just walk away empty-handed; not with my sisters and cousins involved. I had to get some money and in the best case scenario the orchard too. I had slowly come to realize the orchard was worth something. I didn't know how much for sure, but when my dad talked about owning land, it was always a big deal. From what I gathered, people saved their whole lives for a plot as big as the orchard. But maybe Mrs. Nelson had forgotten or changed her mind about giving it up. One particular conversation we had made me bite-my-lip nervous. She had let me in one hot July day, a day after Sam and I had sprayed. The Diazinon smell was still in my nose, and my head ached a little. As I was showing her how the apples were beginning to look fatter on the top than on the bottom, she looked at me and asked, "Are you having fun, then?"

I didn't know what to say. I could think of a lot of words to describe what I was having, but "fun" wouldn't really pop out. I thought of our freezing fingers, stinking shoes, sleepless nights, and poison showers. Then I smiled and simply said, "Yes."

"Good!" she said. "I'm glad. Even if you don't make any money, at least you're having fun. And learning something too. Like the time you dug up my hydrangeas. I'll bet you'll never do something like that again after the lesson I gave you. Sometimes things don't turn out like we hope, but we have to look on the bright side and appreciate the experience."

The hydrangeas. I had tried to forget them, but the whole scene recrystallized. She refused to pay me and kept yelling, "Stupid! Stupid!" If I didn't count my dad, it was the first time an adult had ever said anything like that to me. The next time I saw her, she acted like nothing had even happened and I was supposed to work on her yard again. Hydrangeas. Stupid. I looked at Mrs. Nelson and put my hands up to my face with the palms facing her. I wanted to show her the calluses and blisters I had earned as part of the latest experience. I don't think she got it.

It was strange, but the less contact I had with Mrs. Nelson, the friendlier her son, Tommy, became. When he drove out to see his mom, he would often walk over and talk to me or Amy if he saw us in the orchard. At first, it seemed as if he was inspecting us, but eventually he acted sincerely impressed by what we had done. He had even bothered to learn the names of my sisters and younger cousins. He stopped by right after Sam had done his discing and found us repairing some of the little ditches Sam had destroyed.

"My old man would have really gotten a kick out of this. It's never looked this clean!" Tommy called to us as he came walking up.

"Thanks," I replied, and I had to agree with him. The tops of the trees themselves were a bright green. The ground around them was a rich wet brown with manure peppered over it. Against the bare earth, the trunks looked strong and wide. If you bent low, you could see from one end of the orchard to the other through the weedless space.

"Didn't it look like this when your dad was working on it?" I asked Tommy seriously.

"Nah. I don't think so. It was always more of a hobby to him than anything else. Sometimes he'd just quit doing anything out here in the middle of the year."

"Really?" I replied, and scanned his face to make sure he was telling the truth. He wasn't even smiling, just turning his head around and looking at the trees. "Tommy, would you like to help us water or something one of these times?" I asked him hopefully.

He laughed a little. "Me? Oh, I don't think I'd be very good at it. I'm sure my mom has told you that a hundred times."

"But you helped your dad sometimes, right? So you've seen how everything is done."

He laughed again. "I helped a little but not very will-ingly. I don't think I'm much of a farmer."

"That's what my dad says about himself."

"Maybe it skips a generation."

He walked back to his car and zoomed off. For no particular reason, Michael pulled a small apple off a tree and threw it at the cloud of dust Tommy left.

Chapter 12
DUMP BOXES AND THEY'RE ALL MINE

August apples are dangerous. They're smaller than a baseball and just the right weight for throwing. Sam and Michael had been working on their arms all summer, and I was constantly avoiding shots to my head. An August apple can hurt you in other ways too. Earlier in the summer, they're sour enough to make your lips pucker. But by August, a hint of sweetness emerges that reminds you of that apple's potential. You can forget about the sourness and get way ahead of yourself.

One day Sam and Michael had a contest to see how many August apples they could eat at one time. In our orchard, half of the trees produced green apples and half a green-red combination. They chose the all-green ones. Sam won by eating twelve. Even before he was finished, he was complaining that his stomach hurt. He and Michael spent the next two days moaning and running back and forth to the bathroom.

After the green apple experience, Lisa became very upset about what she called "wasting apples." "All the apple throwing and eating till you're sick is like throwing money away," she lectured. "Think about how much each apple is worth. Jackson, how much is each apple worth?"

I looked back at her like she had asked me to build a TV. I had no idea how much an apple was worth. All I knew was we needed enough of them to add up to the $8,000 that the contract said I owed Mrs. Nelson.

"And I've been thinking, who are we going to sell these apples to, anyway?" she continued.

I had been wondering the same thing and couldn't put the topic off much longer.

"Maybe to the supermarkets or something," I suggested, watching how the others would react to the idea.

"I think supermarkets get their food from places like California," said Amy.

"We could sell them to an apple juice company," offered Sam.

"Or sauce," said Michael.

"Yeah, maybe," I said, trying to sound very thoughtful.

"Why don't you ask Brother Brown where he sells his?" asked Lisa.

"Why would he want to tell us that?" Amy asked quickly. "If we did the same thing, that would be competition and he'd lose money."

I figured she must be right. It was hard for me to think of Brother Brown as competition, but maybe it would be wrong to ask him about selling apples.

"I think we should start with the supermarket, then. Some of us could go with my mom and check things out," I said. By some of us, I really meant Amy and me, but when I asked my mom about it, Lisa and Jennifer insisted on coming too. We went on my mom's regular shopping day, and Amy got to sit in the front seat of the car.

There were a few different supermarkets in Farmington, but my mom always went to Safeway. While she started to load up her grocery cart, the girls and I went to find the produce department.

"I've never noticed before how many different kinds of apples there are," said Lisa as she examined the stacks of fruit in different colors. "What kind do you think ours are?"

"Half are green, so maybe Granny Smith or Golden Delicious. The red ones, I don't know, maybe McIntoshes," said Amy as she ran her fingers over them.

"Look for someone we can talk to," I whispered to Amy.

"How about that guy," she said loudly, and pointed to someone stacking up potatoes about fifty feet away.

We walked closer to him and noticed that he was young, maybe just out of high school. He wore a neat apron and sort of hummed or whistled to himself as he stacked.

"We want to talk to you about your apples," Amy said boldly from behind him. He swung around, and Amy, Lisa, Jennifer, and I were standing in a line staring at him.

"Uh . . . what?" he asked, looking confused.

"Can you tell us where you get your apples?" Amy asked loudly.

"I don't know, maybe Washington. They grow lots of apples there."

"Do they just arrive in a big truck or something? Do you have a big pile of them in the back?" Amy continued.

The potato guy laughed. "No, they come in boxes like this," he said, kicking a box of pears with his foot. "That's a bushel."

"So how much would you pay for a bushel of apples?" Lisa broke in.

"Don't ask me, I just put 'em out."

"How many apples in a box?"

"Mmmm. Maybe a hundred."

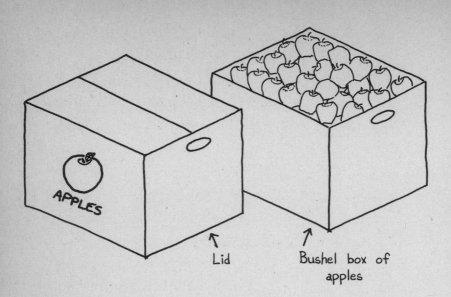

Lid

Bushel box of
apples

"Do you ever sell any apples grown around here?" I
asked.

"I wouldn't be able to tell. If you guys really want to
know, I could get my manager. He does more of the
ordering and that kind of stuff."

"Okay," said Amy quickly.

He walked toward the back of the store and in a few
minutes came back with another man who must have
been the manager. He was middle-aged, with pale skin
and very dark hair combed to one side.

"I hear you want to buy a truckload of apples," the
manager said as he walked up. He was trying his best
to be funny, but he sounded more like a bad actor in a
school play.

Amy looked at him and frowned. "Actually, we thought we'd sell *you* a truckload of them," she said.

The manager stared at her, wearing a creepy grin. He moved his eyes up and down her until she looked away.

I decided I should speak up. "Do you ever buy locally grown fruit and vegetables to sell here?"

"Nope!" he said, still looking at Amy. "All of it comes from our central distributor. Can't be sure that anything else would be safe or high quality."

"We've got a lot of apples that are really high quality, and we've been spraying for worms and bugs regularly."

The manager finally turned and looked at me. "Look, this isn't some kind of flea market. We can't just go buying any old thing off the street. And where are your parents? Shouldn't they be worrying about selling the family crops?" He giggled to himself.

"Then can we talk to the distributor or something? Maybe call him?" I asked hopefully.

"Go ahead if you can find the number. Now, I've got to get back to some real work," he said. He took one last long look at Amy and turned and slumped off slowly, as if he were hoping we would beg him to come back.

When he left, the young potato guy turned to us. "Sorry about that. He wasn't much help."

"Not really," I agreed. "You don't happen to have that distributor's number, do you?"

"No, but maybe you could look in the phone book

or something or call the main line to the store and ask."

"We'll try it," I said. "Do you think we can have a couple of those extra boxes?" I asked, pointing to some boxes he had finished unloading.

"Sure, go ahead," said the potato guy.

We collected as many empty boxes as we could, including a few apple boxes. We also wrote down what Safeway was charging per pound for apples: fifty cents. The side of the apple box said there were forty pounds per bushel, so we had a pretty good idea of what a bushel of apples would cost at Safeway. It was close to the $25 Mrs. Nelson had mentioned when she was talking me into the orchard idea.

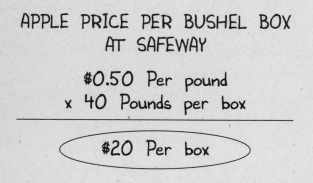

APPLE PRICE PER BUSHEL BOX
AT SAFEWAY

$0.50 Per pound
x 40 Pounds per box
_____

$20 Per box

All of our collected boxes plus Mom's groceries wouldn't fit in the trunk of the car, so we had to ride home with a few of them crammed under our feet and on top of our laps. It was depressing to think about not having a place to sell our apples, and everyone was quiet in the car, staring out the windows.

It's funny how sometimes you can see a thing hundreds of times and never notice it. Then one day you really look at it, and it becomes the only thing you can see. That happened to me just as we were leaving Farmington. On the side of the road, people were selling something out of the back of their car. They had a little sign that said BEANS AND MELONS. All of a sudden, I remembered seeing that car almost every time we went to town.

"Hey, Mom," I asked, "would you ever buy fruit from someone selling it on the side of the road?"

She thought for a few seconds. "Well, maybe. It would probably depend on who was selling it, what it looked like."

"Would you pay the same price that you would in the supermarket?" I asked.

"No, because it would require an extra stop. So it would have to cost less. Why?"

"Just kind thinking," I replied.

I noticed several more cars selling fruit before we got to Fruitland. I saw someone with a WATERMELONS sign in the distance and asked my mom if we could stop.

"I don't want any watermelons," she said.

"I just want to talk to them a little bit."

She pulled off and said she would wait for five minutes.

I had Amy do most of the talking. We found out that the watermelon sellers were a mother and young daughter. They were selling watermelons now but would sell all kinds of fruits and vegetables during the summer and fall. They raised some of it themselves and would drive out of state to buy things like oranges.

"Do you sell things by the pound?" I asked.

"No, by the box," the woman answered.

"I think that settles that," I said, walking back to the car.

"What settles what? What are you talking about?" asked Amy.

"How we're going to sell our apples."

"You're going to have that lady sell our apples?"

"No, we're going to do it ourselves. Just on the side of the road."

"That's all I need, my friends driving by while I'm out on the road."

"It's going to take a lot of boxes," I continued, ignoring her.

———————

The next day Michael and I drove down to General Supply to find out if we could buy cardboard boxes there. I waited until Jimmy was by himself before cornering him.

"You need some more poison already?" he asked when he saw me.

"No, I came down looking for something else. Do you have any cardboard boxes?"

"There are some in the back that we usually just break up when they're empty."

"No, not those kind of boxes. Well, I guess they are cardboard and everything, but I mean boxes for packing fruit into."

"Oh, boxes you would buy, then?"

"Yes. Maybe. If they aren't too expensive."

"I think we order boxes for people. Let me go ask Mr. Sherwood."

He disappeared toward the front of the store and came back carrying a piece of paper. "He says we can order them for people, but they take a while. Here's the form you have to fill out. They even say 'Grown in New Mexico,' and you can check the box here for what kind of fruit you want." Jimmy handed me the form.

"How much are they?" I asked.

"For apples, right?" he asked, and pointed on the form to a little box next to APPLE. "Looks like a $1.50 a box."

"Wow," I said slowly while I looked down at the form. "How long does it take to get them?"

"Six weeks."

"And I have to pick them up here?"

"No, we can have them dropped off at your house."

"Okay, thanks. I'll have to figure all this out. I'm not even sure how many I need. Can I take this form?"

"Yeah, just bring it back when you've decided."

My head was swimming with numbers: price per bushel, price per box, apples per dollar. I had no idea how many boxes we even needed, maybe 100, maybe 10,000. I would have to go home and figure this out together with the person I trusted most with math—Lisa.

Her eyes lit up when I explained the problem.

"Okay, we first have to start by getting a count of all the apples, and then we'll figure out how many boxes we need," she said rapidly.

"No, I want to start by saying if we want to make $8,000, how many boxes do we need to sell," I said. Then I thought about how much the boxes cost, and the spray and cans of pop. We also needed to clear well over $8,000 so I would have something for my sisters and cousins after paying off Mrs. Nelson. "Maybe $12,000."

"Why $12,000?" she asked, amazed by the number.

"I just think it's a really good goal. Something we should be able to do."

"Okay, sounds good to me," she readily agreed. "How much will we charge per box?"

"I don't know. I wonder how many boxes we could pick?"

"That's what I wanted to figure out first."

"No, you wanted to count all the apples."

"It's basically the same thing."

"No, it's not."

We argued back and forth for about an hour. Eventually we did go out and try to count the apples—at least on one tree, which had 300 apples growing on it, relying on our multiplication skills to compute the whole orchard.

Given what the potato guy at Safeway had guessed about the number of apples in a bushel, we estimated we'd get three bushels per tree. Figuring out what we would charge per bushel was much harder, although we knew it had to be a lot less than Safeway's price. After two days of adding, dividing, and multiplying, we decided 1,000 boxes would be about right. It seemed like a lot, but we both liked having a nice round number.

NUMBER OF BUSHEL BOXES NEEDED

How many boxes worth of apples can orchard produce?

$$
\begin{array}{r}
300 \text{ Trees} \\
\times\ 3 \text{ Boxes per tree} \\
\hline
900 \text{ Boxes}
\end{array}
$$

Because each tree could probably produce more than 3 boxes, let's round up to 1,000 boxes.

Goal is to make $12,000:

$12,000 Money target
÷ 1,000 Boxes

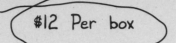

$12 Per box

This would be less than what Safeway
charges ($20). 1,000 boxes
seems like a good goal.

Still, at $1.50 per box that meant $1,500 to buy the 1,000 boxes, and to make $12,000 we would have to sell a bushel for $12. Could we sell that many apples? I agonized over the box form. I didn't dare ask my parents' advice because they might dig a little too deep into the $12,000 target and how I planned to buy the boxes from General Supply. I would have liked to ask Brother Brown, but Amy said he was our competition. I asked my aunt what she would pay for a bushel of apples and all she said was "Nothing. I'll get them from you."

The next morning, I was about to check the box next to APPLE and write 1,000 next to it when my mom called to me.

"Jackson, do you think you can use the tractor and haul off some stuff to the dump for me?"

"You can't take the car?" I asked.

"Some of the stuff is too big to fit in the trunk, like that old chair in the corner. I also want to get rid of some of your father's 'treasures' he's been collecting the last few years."

"But I don't think there's enough gas for the tractor."

"I'll give you $5 to do it, and you can buy some gas."

I considered her offer. "Okay, I'll go get Sam to help. He always likes riding on the tractor."

I took her $5, and Sam and I loaded up the wagon. Sam had to sit in back with the junk to keep it from falling out.

The Fruitland dump was a couple of miles off the main highway. The road to the dump was paved at the beginning but quickly turned to dirt and remained that way until it reached its destination, which was a huge pit dug into the ground. The dump was surrounded by brown desolate land that looked very dull compared to the many-colored garbage of the dump. We hit the first flies a few hundred feet away, and they kept getting thicker the closer we got.

"Do you see what I see?" I yelled excitedly to Sam as we got a clear view of the pit.

"That motorcycle? Yeah, that'd be cool to have!" he yelled back, and pointed at a motorcycle frame without an engine or handlebars.

"No, look there!" I yelled, and pointed.

Piled on top of each other in the pit was a mountain of cardboard boxes. I turned off the tractor and ran over to take a look. They were mostly fruit boxes that said things like Arizona ORANGES, California PEARS, and California PEACHES. There were even a few Washington APPLES.

"I can't believe this!" I shouted. "Why would anyone be throwing away all these good boxes?"

Sam didn't share my enthusiasm, but he helped me look through them. You could tell they had been used, but their insides were mostly clean. They still smelled like fruit, which was a welcome difference from the rest of the dump.

"Quick, let's unload the wagon and see how many of these we can stack up on it," I said to Sam.

"But most of them don't say apples. What are we going to do with them, try to trade them or something?"

"I'm hoping people don't care what kind of box the apples come in. Especially people who buy them on the side of the road."

In an hour we had the wagon stacked high with towers of boxes. Sam found an old roll of twine someone had thrown away, and we tied down the stack. It leaned to one side, but I thought it would probably last until we got home.

"I'll bet we can be back here in less than an hour for

another load," I said as we both jumped back on the tractor. Right then I could see two cars making their way toward the dump. I looked back at the remaining boxes in the pit.

"Hey, Sam," I whispered loudly, "how about staying here and guarding the rest of the boxes so no one gets them?"

He looked around the dump, then back at me. "Do you really think we need to guard them?" he asked with a painful look on his face.

"Do you realize how much these are worth? Please just stay, and if anyone looks interested in them, say they're ours. I'll be back as fast as I can and bring Michael to help."

"Okay," he said, and reluctantly dragged himself toward the pile. I waved goodbye, and he waved back half-heartedly. I put the tractor in third gear and drove as fast as I could back home.

I parked the wagon and tractor between our houses and ran inside both of them to find Michael and the girls. In a few minutes, we were throwing boxes on the ground and pushing them out the back of the wagon. Hardly stopping to catch my breath, I explained to the girls that they should start stacking up the boxes while Michael and I went for more.

As we got to the dump, my heart raced when we

didn't see Sam anywhere. But as soon as he heard the tractor, he popped out of the pile of boxes almost like he was hiding inside.

"Look, I brought Michael to help!" I yelled to him. "Did anyone try to take any?"

"No," Sam replied. "It seemed like you took three or four hours."

"No way! I drove that tractor as fast as it would go."

We stacked boxes again and used the same roll of twine to hold them in place. When I got on the tractor for the return trip, they both got on beside me.

"Somebody needs to stay and guard those boxes. We need a thousand, and I don't want someone stealing any from us," I said.

"Why don't you do it, then?" challenged Michael.

"How about if you both stay and keep each other company. Then you won't have to help with the unloading. It'll be easy," I replied.

They weren't very happy about the plan, and I practically had to push them off the tractor. They shouted something at me as I drove off.

I dumped the load of boxes as quickly as possible and even brought a jug of water back to the dump with me. Sam and Michael drank it greedily and complained about being starved.

This time when we finished tying the boxes down,

Sam and Michael ran for the tractor and Sam sat in the driver's seat.

"We've been talking, and we've decided that if you want anyone to guard those boxes, it has to be you," Michael said as I reached the tractor.

"Come on, guys," I began.

"I've got to get something to eat, and he's not going to stay alone," said Sam, pointing his thumb at Michael.

"Oh, all right!" I said. "But you better drive fast, Sam. Third gear the whole way. Unload them fast, too, and just get something quick to eat."

"Don't worry, we will," Michael called out, laughing as Sam started the tractor and drove off. I watched them until their trail of dust disappeared over a sandy ridge.

I walked around the edge of the pit to kill time, looking at the once-valuable stuff people had thrown into it. On my fourth pass around, I saw a cloud of dust on the horizon. I hurried over to where the rest of the boxes were. It seemed too soon for Sam and Michael to be coming back, and it turned out to be a station wagon driven by an older man. He backed up to the side of the pit and pushed everything piled in the back of this car out the open tailgate.

He saw me standing by the boxes and walked over. "You okay? You need some help?" he asked sympathetically.

"I'm just watching these boxes so that no one takes them."

He looked at me strangely, said, "Okay," and then drove off.

Two more cars drove up while I was waiting. In one of them was the whole family of Darin Skinner, a kid I knew from school who was a year younger than me. They dumped their garbage, and then Darin's dad came over to me and the boxes. Darin stayed in the car.

"Hey, what are you doing here alone?" his dad asked.

I could feel my face turning bright red. "I'm just, just watching these boxes for someone. They want to use 'em. I'm just keeping an eye on 'em," I spluttered out, trying not to look at his face.

"You sure you don't need a ride or something?"

"Oh, no, I'm okay. It'll be just a few more minutes."

He looked me over, then shrugged his shoulders and walked back to his car. Darin watched me out the rear window as they drove off.

On what seemed like my twentieth time around the pit, I started to get angry. Where were those dummies? I should never have let them take that tractor. Sam was probably in first gear, or they were sitting at home watching TV. Then I started to worry that something had gone wrong, like the tractor breaking down. It had been a while since I had sucked out the fuel line. Maybe they were on the side of the road stranded.

The disgusting smell of the dump made it hard to think of food, but I was beginning to feel weak from not eating anything and my mouth was completely dry. I thought of walking the five miles home and how long it would take me. Instead, I burrowed into the stack of boxes. It was uncomfortable but at least provided some shade from the August sun.

I was drifting off to sleep when I heard the sound of the tractor engine and threw off the boxes on top of me.

"Where have you been?" I demanded when Sam and Michael pulled up.

"We went as fast as we could," said Michael, although he didn't sound very convincing.

Piling up the next stack of boxes was exhausting. When we were done, we all made our way to the tractor.

"They'll probably be okay without us watching them," I said, tilting my head toward the remaining boxes.

Over two days we made eight trips and collected 820 boxes, which the girls stacked up pretty neatly considering that there were many different sizes. I kept telling Lisa it was like a pile of money.

My mom came out and looked at the large stack. Next to it were the tractor and wagon, the plow, disc, irrigation barrel, ladders, and all the other equipment we had taken from Mr. Nelson's shed. "This feels like I'm living next to a freight yard. Next thing I know there'll be an actual train running through here." She thought that sounded clever and so was continually telling me to clean up my "freight yard" after that.

———————⊣

Sam, Michael, and I made a trip to General Supply a few days later. We had to buy more Diazinon, and we also bought some rolls of plastic that we used to cover up our boxes in case of rain. "Oh, and, Jimmy," I said as he was adding the poison and plastic to our bill, "I brought back the form for the boxes." I unfolded it and handed it to him.

"Two hundred apple," he said as he looked over the form. "I thought you had like three hundred trees. Is this going to be enough?"

"That should do it. We got some others from another supplier," I replied.

He looked up from the paper. "How much were they?"

"A lot cheaper," I said. "So can we charge those two hundred? And throw in a case of pop." I saw Michael smile out the corner of my eye.

Chapter 13
MONEY JARS

With the boxes in place and the apples hanging fat on
the trees, Lisa and Jennifer embraced the idea of selling
them. They cut out red letters from some of my mom's
sewing material to spell APPLES and glued them on a
white background, making a kind of banner you could
see from a hundred yards away. These type of projects
usually produced crooked letters of random sizes, but
this time the letters were shockingly straight, and the A
was almost the same height as the S.

Amy convinced her dad to push the '68 Chrysler station wagon he had recently given up on out to the road.

This was going to serve as our apple sales headquarters. We would keep the banner inside at night along with any unsold boxes of apples.

"How many thousand dollars are we going to make again?" Amy asked playfully.

I hesitated. "At least a couple thousand each," I replied cheerfully. I thought about Mrs. Nelson's $8,000 and how much we'd have to clear to be left with even $1,000 to divide between the rest of us. "Maybe that's just a best-case scenario, though," I added, not wanting to sound like a total liar.

I took Sam over to Mr. Nelson's shed to look for bags we could use for picking. I remembered seeing in the apple book pictures of people picking with sacks hanging at their sides. In one of the corners, we found two canvas bags that looked like what I was hoping for. They had long straps that fit over your neck so the bag hung at your side. There were metal frames at the tops to keep the bags open and at the bottom little clasps to either close the bags or allow apples to be poured out.

The only thing we needed was ripe apples. They looked the right size and were now more sweet than sour, but I needed an expert opinion as to whether anyone would buy one. The day after the boxes from the dump were stacked, we started watching Brother Brown's orchard to see when he would start picking. Once each day, one of the six of us would walk or ride a bike down to steal peeks through his rows of trees. We were all supposed to act very casual as we went by so he wouldn't suspect us of spying. August was almost over and we hadn't spotted any action.

It finally became too much for me, and I decided to ask Brother Brown directly. I wasn't going to ask him about prices or customers or anything. I just wanted to know when to start picking, something more in the category of general knowledge than competition.

I picked one green apple and one red apple and put them in a paper sack. I spent a whole hour walking the orchard to find the biggest ones we had. After Sunday school, I took my sack up to the front and displayed the apples to Brother Brown.

"Could you take a look at these?" I began. "Couple of average apples from our trees."

Brother Brown looked down at them. "Where are the stems?" he asked abruptly.

"The stems?" I replied in surprise. "I guess still on the tree. I just pulled these off."

"You never pick an apple without the stem. Goes bad faster," he said gruffly.

I blushed with embarrassment. "I'm sorry."

He grunted in return.

"Can you tell me what kind of apples they are?" I asked, trying to move beyond discussing stems.

He looked at me in disbelief. I turned even redder.

"Golden Delicious," he said, pointing at the green apple, and "Roman Beauty," pointing at the red.

"Roman Beauty," I repeated. "I've never heard of those."

Brother Brown gave another little grunt as if to say he wasn't surprised.

"So, are they ready for picking?" I asked eagerly.

"Nope," he said without hesitation.

"Will you tell me when we can start, then?"

"Yeah, I'll let you know."

That was the end of our conversation, but for the rest of the week, I wished I would have asked him to call or something when it was time. There was only a week left before school started, and it was torture to just sit around during the day. I practiced wearing the picking bag and climbing the ladder to reach the highest apples. We also kept up the watering and spraying, although I figured those activities would be abandoned once we started picking.

———⟶

Brother Brown didn't say anything the next Sunday, and we started back to school without having sold or picked a single apple. As much as I usually hated returning to school, that year it was even worse. I didn't even feel that excited about seeing my friends again. My classes seemed like a waste of time, and everyone around me acted so young and immature. By my final period, I had to hold myself into my desk. I wanted to jump up and scream, "I've got real work to do!" and run home to the orchard.

It made me angry that my cousins and sisters didn't share my frustration. When we got off the bus, Amy went on and on about how great high school was.

"The lockers are so much bigger than in junior high, and everyone just seems cooler. The teachers aren't as strict either. My English teacher, Mr. Rodrique, he . . ."

I let her keep babbling without really listening. Lisa had just moved up to sixth grade, and I also had to endure her descriptions of how great that was and how much responsibility the kids were given. I didn't waste my breath correcting her. Plus, I knew I had to stay on her good side.

In the middle of the week, I went into her room after dinner for a serious talk. I tried to make it clear it was serious by closing the door.

"What are you reading?" I began as I sat on her bed.

"Just reading ahead a little in my social studies book," she replied without looking up.

I shifted nervously on the bed. "Are you excited to start getting some of the apples sold?"

"Sure," she said, looking up in suspicion. She could already tell I wanted something. "Why wouldn't I be?"

"No reason. I'm just glad you're so enthusiastic, even making the sign. I just figured you'd be in charge of all the sales and counting the money and stuff."

She closed her book. "Yeah, that's what I was thinking too. I was even planning out a system."

"Then you can definitely be in charge."

She smiled and looked thoughtfully out the window.

"The only thing is," I said reluctantly, "I don't think we have a lot of time to get them all picked and sold."

"Yeah, so?"

"It's just that we're probably going to have to sell on Saturdays and after school. I know that before the summer you didn't like to work after school, but we really, really need you now. And it will only be until we finish picking."

Her mouth sunk into a frown as I was talking. I could tell she was thinking hard, but she didn't say anything.

"I know you're smart enough that you can do any homework during class or at night after it's dark. And just for a few weeks," I added.

"I could keep track of all the money and keep it in my room?" she finally asked.

"Of course, you'd be in charge of it."

She tapped an empty glass jar she had on the little table in her room. "Okay, then," she agreed.

———

On Saturday I convinced myself three different times that I was going to start picking without Brother Brown's clearance. Each time I climbed up the ladder and reached for an apple, I couldn't bring myself to pull it off the branch.

I finally found the courage to pluck six large golden apples and then assembled my cousins and sisters.

"Take a bite. Tell me if they're ready," I demanded.

Sam and Michael attacked their apples until juice ran down their necks. The girls were more delicate, closing their eyes to evaluate every bite.

"Best apple I've ever had," Amy concluded. "Crisp, but not too hard. Just the right amount of sweet."

Everyone else nodded their heads.

"They're not going to get any better, right?" I asked, savoring the apple I'd eaten halfway through.

"They couldn't," replied Sam proudly. "I think we made them perfect."

———

During Sunday school the next day, I kept hoping Brother Brown would make a special announcement about the beginning of the harvest or something. Instead, he just dully droned on about epistles and parables. When it was over, I waited until the other kids had left the room. He didn't even look at me. I kicked my chair in frustration as I got up to leave. Who cared what he thought? Those apples were ready, and I was picking on Monday. When I reached the door, I heard Brother Brown's voice behind me.

"Better get goin' on those Goldens," he said calmly.

I swung around. "It's time, then?"

"Romes will keep awhile so start with the Goldens."

"Thanks for telling me," I said in a relieved voice. "I kind of thought they were ready. Uh . . . how long do we have?"

"Five, six weeks maybe."

"What happens after that?"

"No good for most people. Cows like 'em."

———————

I assembled my sisters and cousins that night for a strategy meeting. We had had these before, but there seemed to be an extra importance to this one. It felt to me like we were packing up and leaving home.

"We're going to need a few boxes to take up to the road, so maybe tomorrow we can all help with picking and then start selling on Tuesday," I began when everyone was listening.

"Who's going to be selling and who's going to be picking?" asked Michael.

I looked them all over. "Amy and I will pick using the bags since we're the tallest. I was thinking Lisa and Jennifer would do the selling. We'll probably need more help with picking, though, so Sam and Michael can you stay out in the orchard?"

"I wanted to sell," complained Michael.

"Why, 'cause you think it'll be easier?" teased Amy.

"No, 'cause I'd be good at it," Michael said, giving Amy a dirty look.

"Don't worry, you'll probably get a chance to. We have a few weeks to go, but we first have to concentrate on picking. And, Sam, maybe you could be in charge of driving the boxes up to the road."

Sam happily agreed and Michael insisted he should ride along to help.

After the plans had been made and the meeting broke up, Amy approached me alone. "This whole thing has been fun and everything," she said while grinning sarcastically, "but how much longer do you expect us to keep working?"

"Brother Brown says we only have a few weeks until the apples are too old, so it can't be longer than that. Why, do you have another job or something?"

"No, but I would like to have a social life now that I'm in high school. That's kind of hard when you're out in the fields working for your cousin all day and night."

"I promise it won't be much longer." I tried to think of more things to say that would be encouraging and inspiring, like how much money she was going to make, but there was always that possibility of making zero. I couldn't really promise anything, but I needed her to stick with me a little longer.

——————

After school on Monday, we hauled boxes out to the orchard, and Amy and I put on the picking bags. I climbed to the top of a ladder and turned around to face everyone. "Okay, it's very important to pick them with the stems still on. Don't just pull. You have to be careful. Everyone but me and Amy will stay low and take their own box and fill it."

There were mumbles of agreement. I turned around and grabbed my first apple. I pulled its stem but discovered it took a kind of twisting motion to get it off the branch. It was definitely harder than just yanking on the bottom of the apple. It took about ten minutes to pick all of them within my reach. I looked over at Amy. She seemed to be naturally twisting and pulling without much effort. I moved my ladder over to hers.

"How's it going?" I called over to her. "Having any trouble with the stems?"

"No, not really," she answered casually.

I continued to watch and tried to imitate her hands. No matter how much I tried, I never seemed to be able to balance like her. I had to constantly grab on to branches to keep from tipping over. After another ten minutes, my bag was full and pulling me over to one side. I lowered myself carefully down the ladder and walked toward the nearest box. Placing the bag inside, I unclamped the latch at the bottom and let the apples spill out. There was a satisfying rolling and thumping sound as they hit the bottom of the box, which ended up about two-thirds full.

Before going back up the ladder, I walked around to see how the others were doing. Lisa and Jennifer were very carefully removing single apples at a time from the tree and placing them in a box. They were painfully slow but paying attention to their stems.

Michael's box was almost full. I looked through the apples inside.

"Where are the stems? Not one of them has a stem!" I said very loudly.

"It's easier to pick them without stems," he said with a shrug.

"Yeah, I know it's easier, but it's the wrong way! Lisa, remember this box. It's the one that says 'pears.' You should try to sell this first so they don't sit around very long. And please, Michael, pick them with the stems!"

I looked over at Sam, who had been watching with a guilty look on his face. When I saw his almost-full box, I could see he had a good mix of apples with and without stems. I looked at him, shaking my head.

"I'll be more careful," he said, looking away.

"It is kind of hard," I replied. "The girls seem to be better at it."

We continued working around the first three trees until they were almost cleared of apples. By the time it got dark, we had filled sixteen boxes with Golden Delicious, which had turned from green to a yellow-green color.

"I'm starving," said Amy, and that was the cue for everyone to stop working.

I left my bag on a ladder. "I guess that's a pretty good start and we got a lot more boxes per tree than I was expecting. At least you'll have something to sell tomorrow," I said to Lisa.

"What price are we going to start with, then?" Lisa asked.

This felt like a very big decision. It all seemed like guessing and hoping. "Let's go with $12 like we talked about and see what happens."

———————⟶

On Tuesday we all helped load the sixteen boxes on the wagon and walked alongside as Sam drove the tractor to the road. Lisa unrolled her banners and set them up next to the car, and we arranged a few boxes facing the road with their tops off.

"Okay, well, this is it," I announced. "We're ready for customers. It kinda feels like we need a drum roll or a ribbon to cut."

"So good luck, you guys," said Amy, cutting me off. She waved to Lisa and Jennifer, and then started walking toward the orchard. "I'm getting off the road before my friends see me."

"Just yell if you need anything or have any problems," I said, trailing Amy.

"So $12, right?" Lisa asked.

"Yeah," I replied, shrugging.

Amy, Michael, and I followed the tractor back into the orchard and started picking again. "You sure the girls can handle everything by themselves? I mean Lisa's only eleven, and that could be a lot of money," said Amy.

I gave her a troubled look. "I'm sure she can keep track of it all. As long as someone doesn't try to steal it," I muttered. It was something else to worry about.

We kept listening for what might be happening up at the road, straining to hear any cars pulling over. After about thirty minutes, the suspense became too much.

"Michael, go find out if anyone has stopped and if they've sold anything," said Amy.

Michael ran off eagerly to check while we waited nervously. I was having even more trouble than usual keeping the apples attached to the stems. In a few minutes, Michael came back breathing hard from running. "Three people stopped, but nobody bought anything."

No one was sure how to take the news. Was it more important that people were stopping or that no one was buying? "Okay, thanks," I said. "We'll have to send you back every once in a while." Michael ran back and forth about every thirty minutes. On his third trip, he reported the first sale and we all gave a little cheer.

"Hope it was that pear box," I said, smiling at him.

The second sale didn't come until a couple of hours later, about the time we decided to pack things up for the night. We drove the tractor back up to the road and greeted Lisa and Jennifer.

"So how was it?" asked Amy. "We heard you sold two boxes," she said encouragingly.

"Well, for one thing, we didn't have any change," said Lisa. "We could have probably sold another two or three more if we would have had change."

"Oh man, I didn't even think about that," I groaned.

"Yeah, I know," Lisa replied in an irritated voice. "Another thing is that everyone said that someone else was selling them down the road for $8, so we might have to lower our price."

"How many would you have sold for $8?" asked Amy.

"Probably a lot more," Lisa answered.

"Well?" Amy asked, looking over at me.

It was an easy calculation: charging $8 per box for a thousand boxes would not cover the $8,000 plus expenses. All the money we earned would go straight to Mrs. Nelson, and we'd end up with nothing, not even the orchard. Then again, if no apples sold, we wouldn't even get close. "Let's try $8 tomorrow, then," I said. Since the trees seemed to have produced more apples than I anticipated, if we could just get more boxes, maybe we could push past the $8,000.

"Did people like the apples, though, when they saw them?" asked Amy.

"They seemed to," said Lisa. "The Navajos called them white apples, and they wanted to check the box to make sure we didn't put wormy ones at the bottom."

Fruitland was right across the river from the Navajo Indian reservation, so there were lots of Navajos driving back and forth on Highway 550 in front of our house. They would be a large percentage of our customers, so it was important that they liked the apples.

"Some people asked for a sample, but I didn't know what to say," Lisa continued.

"I think you should just give them one and let them try," said Amy.

I nodded in agreement.

"Let's try to borrow some money from our parents tonight so we can get change. It sounds like we can sell a lot more with the right price and with change," Amy concluded with a little anticipation in her voice.

We rolled up the banners and stuck them into the station wagon along with as many apple boxes as would fit. The rest we loaded behind the tractor and drove back home.

My mom agreed to lend us ten $1 bills for Wednesday, and my aunt lent us five more. Before going to bed, I made a sign out of a piece of cardboard that said $8.

——————⌐

On Wednesday afternoon business was a lot different. While Amy and I picked, Michael ran back and forth with reports. Within the first hour, four boxes had sold and then six in the next. Sam had to pile more boxes into the wagon and take them up to the road. Amy and I kept guessing as to how many boxes would be sold by the end of the day. At dusk we threw the picking bags on the ladders and walked out to the road.

Lisa looked flustered but happy. "Today was much better!" she said when she saw us.

"So how many did you sell?" asked Amy.

"Twenty!" replied Jennifer.

"The price made a big difference," said Lisa. "We also started letting people taste an apple and that seemed to convince most of them."

"Yeah, that's a good idea," I said, thinking of how sweet they were. "They'll sell themselves. Did anyone care that they aren't in apple boxes?"

"They asked why they weren't, but I don't think it stopped anyone from buying," she replied.

"I hope you didn't tell anyone we got them from the dump," said Amy.

"I just said they came from some other fruit growers," said Lisa.

"If you sell that many every night, we should be done in how long?" asked Amy.

Lisa's eyes drifted up toward the sky as she calculated. "About fifty days."

"How many weeks?" asked Amy.

"Eight if you don't count Sundays," said Lisa.

Amy looked at me the way my mom usually looked at my dad when he forgot their anniversary.

"I'll bet we'll sell a lot more on Saturdays," I said, trying to sound positive. I really hoped we would. The clock in my head was beginning to tick too fast. Eight weeks was too long. According to Brother Brown, we maybe had five weeks before the apples were overripe and no one wanted them.

We pushed the unsold boxes into the station wagon and walked home together. After a hundred feet, Lisa said, "Oh, yeah!" and ran back. She returned carrying a glass jar with money in it. She held it up to show us.

"So is the jar part of your system?" I asked Lisa with a smile.

"Yeah, but just one part," she replied secretively.

Chapter 14
DOUBLE-CROSSING OLD LADY

We quickly discovered that with an $8 price, we could sell apples faster than we could pick them. I told Lisa to try $10 to see if we could get more dollars per box. She reported that sales slowed to a trickle and customers complained that they could buy them cheaper down the road. Years later I learned this had something to do with supply and demand and that people would go to college for four years to learn about it. We didn't know what to call it, but seemed to be stuck with $8 boxes. On Saturday we unloaded all that we had at that price by the early afternoon and moved our salesmen back to the orchard for picking.

Lisa liked to announce running totals every day for the number of boxes sold and dollars collected. She put our weekly total at $720. It was a lot of money for a bunch of kids who had never held a $20 bill before, and Michael knew enough math to let us know we could buy 2,880 candy bars with it. Still, we only had maybe six more weeks to sell, and I knew it wasn't enough per week to come close to $12,000, or even $8,000. In a way, the trees had grown money like Mrs. Nelson predicted. She was going to get it all, though, unless we could pick faster and get more apples out on the road.

That Saturday the new boxes from General Supply arrived on a flatbed truck that drove up to my house. Lisa, Jennifer, and Michael helped stack the new boxes, which were white with bright red lettering that said "New Mexico APPLES." The boxes looked so clean and crisp, they almost seemed too fancy after using the dump boxes. After covering them with plastic, we decided we would save them until all the others were gone.

The arrival of the boxes reminded me that even if we could fill and sell the thousand we started with, at $8 a box there wouldn't be enough money to even pay off Mrs. Nelson after clearing the General Supply bill. By then, I knew that each tree produced at least four boxes of apples, so there was enough in the orchard to fill at least twelve hundred boxes. On the way home from school the next Monday, I was deciding whether to place an order for two hundred more from General Supply when Lisa said, "It's too bad we don't have some smaller boxes too."

"Why?" I asked.

"Because a lot of people don't want a whole bushel box, and they ask for something smaller."

"Really? Like how many apples do they want?"

"Maybe a dozen. I guess like what you would put in one of those plastic bags that you use at the grocery store."

"Hmm. So do you think they would buy them in those kinds of bags?"

"Probably."

When my sisters and cousins had all gathered around the old station wagon later that night, I brought up the possibility of using the bags.

"They're just sitting out at the supermarket. Why don't we just get some there? They don't charge you for them," said Amy.

"But we would need hundreds. Don't you think they'd care?" I asked.

"Can't hurt to try and see how many we could get," said Amy. "Someone should go with one of our moms the next time they go to town."

"Okay, who?" I asked.

Amy looked around. "Michael, because he wouldn't be afraid of anyone working there."

Michael didn't disagree, and it was decided he would go with my aunt the next time she went grocery shopping. When my aunt heard the plan, she thought it was funny and even agreed to make a special trip the next day. She mentioned something about paying Safeway back for their high prices and agreed to give Michael time to collect bags by staying extra long.

———

After school on Tuesday, the two of them left for town, and the rest of us started picking and selling. Michael returned about two and a half hours later and ran out into the orchard with plastic bags clenched in his fists.

"I got 'em!" he yelled as he ran up to us. "Look!"

"How many did you get?" asked Amy.

"I don't know," said Michael, "a lot, though. At first I thought of just taking a couple of rolls, you know still rolled up. But I didn't think they would let me out of the store that way."

"So what did you do?" I asked.

"I just started tearing them off the roll one at a time. I figured once they were torn off, no one else would want to use 'em, so they wouldn't stop me."

"So you just stood there tearing off bags? Didn't anyone say anything?" asked Amy.

"Whenever anyone came close to me, I would move so they couldn't see what I was doing," Michael said very proudly.

"And you went through the checkout line with all the bags?" I asked.

"Yeah, with my mom."

"Did the checker say anything?" I asked.

"She asked what all the bags were for, and I told her I needed them for a project and said, 'They're free, right?' She didn't seem to care."

"Wow, I can't believe you did it," I said. "Take them up to Lisa and tell her to see how many bags you can fill from a box."

Michael ran up to the road and then came back about half an hour later. "She says about fourteen or fifteen bags for a box," he said when he returned.

I looked at Amy. "If we sold them for a dollar a bag, that's $14 a box, and we get the box back," I said.

"Sounds good to me," she replied. "Michael, go tell Lisa to try and sell them for a dollar."

"And tell her to really push the bags," I said as he turned to leave.

—————————>

Over the next few days, the bags proved to be a hit. Lisa reported that she sold about two bags for every box. She had also counted all of the bags Michael had taken from Safeway and came up with 715. Soon Sam was bringing empty boxes back to the orchard after they had been used to fill up bags. I hadn't figured out things exactly, but I suddenly was confident that if we could just fill all the bags and boxes, we could at least get past the $8,000 hurdle. Filling them all was going to be a problem, though. I felt like I was picking faster and faster all the time, but there were just not enough hours in the day. With Lisa and Jennifer selling and Sam hauling boxes around, picking came down mostly to Amy, Michael, and me.

I became so obsessed with picking apples that I hardly noticed anything else once I got home from school. This included Mrs. Nelson's house. I had stopped glancing in the windows to see if she was watching us and just raced by on my way home. I could hardly remember the last time I had seen her. I was lost in picking one afternoon during the second week of apple harvesting when her son, Tommy, sneaked up on me. I was concentrating on stems so hard that I didn't hear him until he was standing next to my ladder.

"Hey, Jackson! How's business?" he called to me.

I twisted around to find him staring up at me with a big grin. I hadn't seen him for a while either, so I couldn't hide my surprise. "Pretty good, I guess. Can't pick fast enough though." I eased my way down the ladder and dumped the load of apples from my bag into the nearest box.

"Oh yeah? How many boxes you planning on selling?"

I knew Tommy had seen the contract I signed with Mrs. Nelson, although he had never mentioned it to me. I looked over at Amy, who was one tree away and listening to the radio. I lowered my voice so she wouldn't hear anything if the conversation slipped into details about money and payoffs. "We've got to clear $8,000, so that's gotta mean over a thousand boxes," I said to Tommy with a resigned shrug.

Tommy gave me a knowing smile. "I don't know where she got that $8,000 number."

"She said your dad could make that easily in a year."

Tommy let out a little chuckle. "I doubt he ever made even half that much. My mom doesn't know the difference between $800 and $8,000. She's terrible with money."

My shoulders sagged. "Really? She made it sound, you know, so doable."

"Well, what do you think now? Is it doable?"

I put my head down and looked at my feet. "I guess it has to be. We'll just have to work harder." I looked over at Amy. "I can't just walk away with nothing. I've got to give the other kids something."

Tommy's mouth curved up into a sympathetic grin. "It's kind of a crazy situation."

He said goodbye and lumbered out of the orchard

while I quickly climbed back up my ladder and a new dread hit me. What if Mrs. Nelson had known the $8,000 target was impossible? What if she wanted me to fail all along so she could keep the orchard and the money while playing mind games with her son? I flushed from my neck up, but kept hidden among tree branches so Amy wouldn't notice.

———┐

After school the next day, Mrs. Nelson was waiting for me outside her house as I ran home from the bus stop.

"Jackson? Can you come talk to me for a minute?" she called sweetly.

I skidded to a stop and reluctantly followed her up to her porch. My sisters and cousins stood watching from the dirt lane, but I waved for them to keep walking before trudging through Mrs. Nelson's door.

"Come in, come in," she called, and pointed me into one of her chairs. "Can I get you anything to drink?"

Her sudden friendliness was very transparent. "No thanks."

Mrs. Nelson sat across from me and put on a big smile while she smoothed down her hair and checked that her earrings were in place. "Tommy said he stopped by and watched you pick apples last night."

"Uh-huh," I grunted, nodding my head.

"He said you've got your own little fruit stand up on the road. Said you were determined to make that $8,000.

Now, is that what we agreed on? It seems so long ago. I didn't realize you were taking things so seriously."

"I thought that's what you wanted. I was supposed to prove I was the true heir."

"What I wanted? Oh, I don't think so. I just wanted to see that orchard alive again. You kept pressing me for money. Looking back, it kind of seems like you were taking advantage of me when I was vulnerable." Her broad smile faded and then drooped into a self-pitying frown.

My skin began to get hot. A shock wave of anger almost pushed me out of my chair, but I stayed quiet and looked away from Mrs. Nelson's face.

"Now Tommy thinks we should make a different agreement," she continued. "He thinks we should just split the money no matter how much there is. And I would keep the orchard, of course. I mean it's ludicrous to think of just giving it away to a child. That land's probably worth more than your parents will ever have in their lifetimes."

Her voice had the same sugary sweet tone she had started with, but the words were bitter and resentful. All of a sudden it was like I was trying to steal something from her—something I wasn't good enough to have. She really had hoped I would just give up and go away when she started ignoring me.

"I wanted that in the first place. Just to split the

money," I said in a shaky voice. I spoke slowly, forcing out every word.

"Good. Then let's say you can have twenty percent of it. That should be more than enough to make you happy. You're only thirteen."

I sat in the same chair I had in February when she had practically begged me to become the orchard's "true heir." Now she was staring me down through a fake smile and telling me I should be happy with whatever crumbs she threw me. I had done more than she had ever imagined and now she was insulting me. She should be getting 20 percent. No! She shouldn't get anything! She hadn't lifted a finger in that orchard. I couldn't hold the anger back anymore.

"What if I just keep all the money?" I growled, narrowing my eyes menacingly.

Mrs. Nelson jerked back in shock and stared back at me with horrified eyes. "You wouldn't dare! I'd sue you for it! I'd . . . I'd have you arrested for trespassing."

I wanted to reply with something clever about child labor laws and slavery, but my brain was too agitated to get any of that out. "I'd like to see you try!" I grunted, and jumped to my feet.

"You disrespectful brat! You stupid, stupid child!" she stammered.

I rushed to her door and then called back, "We've got a contract! You signed it!"

Once I got out the door, I realized my whole body was shaking. I stumbled around the corner of her house and bent over trying to control my breathing. After five minutes, I ran into the orchard and grabbed my picking bag.

"What did she want?" called Amy from atop a ladder ten feet from me.

"Just wanted to see how the picking was coming," I answered, trying to sound natural.

Amy looked at me suspiciously but didn't ask more questions.

Chapter 15
No Sleep until We're Through

It all came down to the apples. It was as simple as pulling them off the trees and putting them in the boxes. I convinced myself that if we could just do that fast enough, everything would work out. I would simply stick to the contract. Somehow the money and Mrs. Nelson would all work out. It was easiest to only think about the apples.

Amy and Michael picked at a steady pace, although Michael had slowed down trying to be careful with the stems. I borrowed a watch and figured out that between the three of us we could fill about four boxes per hour.

There were about four hours between getting home from school and when it got dark. At sunset everyone automatically headed home for dinner comparing who deserved to be the most tired. During that second week of picking, I decided filling sixteen boxes a day wasn't going to be enough and I had better keep working after dinner. I was afraid to ask anyone else to help, so I grabbed the cheapest lamp I could find in the house and headed back out to the orchard alone. Michael's long line of extension cords was stretched between his house and the trees so we could listen to the radio. I unplugged the radio and plugged in the lamp.

Picking in the near darkness was hard. I had to constantly reposition the lamp to give myself some idea of where apples were on the trees. I lost track of time but could tell it was late by how much my neck and shoulder hurt from holding the picking bag. I filled up five boxes, then grabbed the lamp and dragged myself home. The clock said 11:30 when I walked in the door.

I felt that to have any chance of making the necessary money, we were going to have to pick twenty-five boxes a day. I made it my goal to produce an extra nine boxes every night. After dinner I would grab the light and head out. It took me until two in the morning to get nine boxes picked, and by the third week I had decided I would be better off splitting the extra work between morning and night. I would finish picking at around midnight and then wake up at 5:00 a.m. so I could get a couple of hours of work in before school.

I had never tried to survive on less than five hours of sleep a night before, and it began to suck the life out of me. I had always been smart enough in school that I could finish any homework assignments during class and very rarely had to take anything home to finish. With my new schedule, though, I found myself falling asleep during almost every period. The undone homework piled up, but I figured I would catch up with it when we had finished selling.

In general, I avoided looking at myself much in the mirror, but when I did get a glimpse during those days, I could see my eyes had deep black circles around them. The rest of my face had a sickly color with my nose and the whites of my eyes looking a bloodshot red. My mom complained every night that I was working myself sick and looked awful. "Dan, tell him he has to stop spending so much time out in that orchard," she said to my dad one night. "He's going to kill himself."

"Oh, leave him alone. It's good he has a career he's so interested in," he replied. "He's got to learn what hard work is like. I'm not going to be the one to tell him to stop."

My mom gave him a dirty look and continued to nag me.

During those late nights alone, my mind would wander away from the trees. I began to think that maybe it would be okay to just get 20 percent of the money. At least that was something and I could get some sleep. But I'd have to go beg Mrs. Nelson to reconsider after I'd yelled at her. Even if she didn't slam the door in my face, she'd probably make me take 10 percent or less. It would be humiliating. Tommy might be able to help. He seemed sympathetic enough but hadn't come around again since our last talk. No. My only hope was that contract. If I could just live up to my end of it, someone could enforce it—a judge maybe.

I even thought about getting my parents involved. I knew I couldn't ask them to actually help with the picking without explaining the $8,000 deal. And if that came out, things were bound to get even uglier with Mrs. Nelson. The last thing I wanted was my mom going over to her house screaming wildly about how she was killing her baby and she should give me all the money. My dad would probably just call me an idiot for not taking the job at the scrap yard. My brain hadn't had enough sleep to think about any of it very clearly. It seemed the only thing I could really do was to keep my mouth shut, hope for the best, and pick—pick even harder.

Lisa would make regular announcements about how much money we had made. She giggled in delight as the numbers climbed into the thousands. I tried not to listen, knowing we were falling further and further behind where we needed to be. By the end of week four, I was trying to push out even more boxes and only getting three or four hours of sleep a night. I instantly dozed off in Sunday school when I hit my chair. When class was over, I woke up to Brother Brown shaking me.

"You all right?" he said gruffly.

"What, uh, yeah, just a little tired."

"You look like you fell off a truck."

I forced a smile and walked out with him watching me.

———⟶

On Wednesday of the fifth week, I began to get a little hysterical. During dinner I kept giggling at everything my sisters said and rocking back and forth in my chair. No one would make eye contact with me, and eventually we all sat in silence looking down at our plates.

After dinner I grabbed the lamp and started for the door. Jennifer followed me, putting on a coat and hat.

"I thought you might want some help," she said, looking at me with a worried face.

"Are you sure?" I asked her as I opened the door.

"Yeah, I'm not very good at picking, though."

"That's okay. I've got a better job for you," I said, feeling a little less tired. When we had reached the spot in the orchard where Amy and I had left the ladders, I said, "Here, can you hold up the lamp for me so I can see?"

"Sure," she said, and took the lamp from my hand.

"It's nice to have someone else out here in the dark."

"Do you ever get scared out here alone?"

"I think I feel too tired anymore to feel scared. It takes too much energy."

"So why are you coming out here every night, anyway? We've already made a ton of money. Me and Lisa don't know why you're so obsessed with making more."

I paused before I answered so that I wouldn't say anything dumb, although part of me wanted to confess the $8,000 deal. "I hate to see these apples go to waste or those boxes. I just want to see them all sold."

"I guess I do too," she said.

Picking went a lot faster with her out there holding the light since I didn't have to keep climbing down the ladder to reposition it. I also felt safe somehow listening to her voice telling me about classes at school and what she wanted for Christmas.

After a few hours, she began to fade. Everything went dark all at once. I looked down, and she had dropped to the ground asleep, letting the lamp fall next to her. I didn't know whether to try and wake her up and take her home or not. In the end, I just turned the lamp back over and kept picking, leaving her on the ground. I would take her home after finishing up just a couple more boxes.

A little later I heard footsteps coming through the

darkness. I turned and saw my dad walking up. He looked down at Jennifer and frowned.

"You just going to leave your sister lying here on the ground?" he asked angrily.

"I was about to finish up and bring her in."

"Maybe your mother's right. Why don't you come back home before you make yourself really sick."

"Let me just finish this up."

"Come on, I'm not sure what you're trying to prove here. You're going to hurt yourself and your sisters."

A feeling of resentment swept over me. If he was so worried, why didn't he try and help me finish? He hardly seemed to care if I succeeded. "I'm not trying to prove anything, Dad!" I yelled. "You're the one who's always talking about working so hard! I only started out here because I didn't want to work at that stupid scrap yard! But I can't stop now or you'll call me a quitter! I just wish for once you'd say I was doing something right!" What I said didn't make much sense, but I was so full of anger and frustration that I wanted to scream anything at someone.

My dad just looked at me. I thought he would shout something back, but he didn't. Something close to sympathy came over his face. "Do what you want, then. It's your health," he said. He picked up my sister and carried her home.

I waited until I knew he had reached the house, and then I switched off the lamp and carried it home.

I was exhausted but couldn't sleep peacefully. I kept thinking of yelling at my dad and my little sister lying there on the ground. Deep down I craved for him to say he was proud of me and I was doing something he never could have done when he was my age. That kind of thing would probably never leave his mouth. Maybe the best I could hope for was the fact that he didn't yank me off that ladder when I had yelled at him.

I also thought of Sam's and Michael's faces when I would have to tell them there would be no money for them after all. Mrs. Nelson was going to take everything just like I'd agreed to in the contract. When I did fall asleep, I dreamed that I was picking apples that wouldn't come off their branches. No matter how hard I pulled, they clung to the trees. I woke up in the middle of the night to find myself standing on my bed grasping at the walls of my room as if I were reaching for an apple tree.

$$\longrightarrow$$

Since the picking had begun, the one thing I had come to rely on was Amy's presence. Unexpectedly, during the second week of picking, she had stopped complaining or asking when it was all going to be over. She was out beside me every day until it got dark and all day on Saturdays. Compared to the nights when I was alone, those times hardly felt like work.

She never mentioned me staying up late at night. Maybe she thought that as long as she didn't acknowledge what I was doing, she wouldn't have to feel guilty about not joining me. When we would go out to pick, she would try not to look at the boxes I had finished the night and morning before.

She constantly encouraged me, though, whenever we were together. She would say things like "You know you're going to make more money than anyone else at high school did in their summer job" or "You know that my friend Paige Manning likes you. When this is over, you should call her because the two of you would hit it off." I didn't really believe what she was saying, but it was nice to hear it, anyway. When Sam would come tell us about a problem up at the road, Amy would always run off and handle it, telling me, "You stay here. I'll be right back."

———————⌐

On Thursday afternoon of the sixth week, Amy and I were already picking when Lisa stopped to talk to us on her way out to the road. She had a jelly jar full of green bills in her hands. This was just one jar of an assortment she kept under her bed with different amounts of money inside and labels taped to their outsides.

"I just want you to know that we've now cleared the $5,000 mark," she said excitedly.

"No way! That's amazing," said Amy.

"Yeah, good news," I added. I tried to sound as enthusiastic as possible, even though it was actually terrible news. We had so little time left and were still thousands of dollars away from where we had to be.

"I never really thought we could sell this much," Lisa continued.

I bit my lip and climbed up my ladder. We had moved into the red apple portion of the orchard. Brother Brown called them Roman Beauties, but, according to Lisa, the Navajo customers just called them the "red ones." They didn't like them as much as the Golden Delicious, or "white ones," but were still buying them.

The leaves on the trees had begun to turn from the bright green of summer into the yellow green of fall. They felt leathery instead of soft like when they were new. While we picked, I listened to Amy humming along to the radio and chattering about her homeroom teacher. Everyone else was up at the road. Then I heard a sound I had never heard before. From behind me, there was a low thump. I looked around. Again in the distance, I heard the thump. I strained my ears to listen and heard another one.

My heart raced as I realized what the sound was: apples falling off the trees and hitting the ground.

We had reached the end.

It was probably only a matter of days before the rest

of them were bad. I tried quickening my pace and even stopped worrying about the stems. I threw apples into the picking bag and practically jumped off the ladder to dump them in boxes.

My fingers began to shake from a combination of fear and fatigue. All I could hear were the thump of falling apples and the pop as I pulled others off their stems. The tree became blurry, and I could hardly keep my balance. As I tried to move off the ladder, I slipped and fell to the ground. Apples spilled out of my bag.

I lay with my face in the dirt, breathing it in. I pounded it with my fists over and over and then raised my head up and spit mud from my mouth. I rolled over and looked straight up into the branches of the nearest trees. Then there was Amy standing over me.

I sat up and put my head on my knees, and she sat down on the ground in front of me. She didn't ask what was wrong or if I was hurt. She didn't say anything.

It was warm for October, one of those days that trick you into thinking it's still summer. I felt the sweat from my head making the knees of my pants wet. The sky was changing from dark to light blue, and the first streaks of pink were forming above us. A golden light streamed through the leafy shadows and onto Amy's face. Even the beams of light seemed as if they were moving in slow motion.

"Do you remember when we were first learning to ride bikes?" she asked.

I didn't say anything.

"You could never balance very well," she continued. "But you kept trying over and over again. I remember your legs and arms were like one big bruise and scrape before you figured it out."

I looked at her silently.

"And then when I went to kindergarten, you would ride your bike out to the bus every day to meet me. I always liked that. I still remember it really clearly." Her voice trailed off as she tried to picture it in her mind.

"Sometimes I wish we would have been in the same grade, though," she said. "You could have probably helped me with most of my classes. Maybe people would think I was smart too." She smiled.

Suddenly, I wanted to tell her everything—to make her understand and to make her forgive me. It wasn't going to be enough! No one was going to get any money. And I had done everything for the wrong reasons and had led them on the whole time. If she would just say it was okay, I could face Sam and Michael and my sisters and all their disappointment. I could accept everything else, as long as at that moment she said it was okay.

"Amy?" I began, my voice cracking. "I should have told you something right from the beginning."

She stared at me without changing her expression.

"I . . . I . . . kind of made this agreement with Mrs. Nelson. I was so stupid!" I said, pounding the ground again.

"I know," she replied, looking down. "She told me."

"What?" I gasped, with my mouth open. "What did she tell you?"

"About the $8,000 and how you would get the orchard."

"When?" I asked, still stunned.

"About a month ago. I think she doesn't really want you to have it anymore and was thinking the rest of us wouldn't help you if we knew about your agreement."

I sat up a little. Amy knew? And she didn't completely hate me? All of a sudden my forehead didn't feel as hot. "So why did you? Why did you keep picking?"

She didn't say anything at first, just grabbed a stick and started drawing on the ground. When she spoke, her voice was clear and calm.

"I never was doing any of it for the money. I never really believed you about making any money."

I smiled back at her weakly.

"Things are so different now from how they used to be," she continued. "Sometimes I get afraid when I think about what's going to happen to me."

"You mean after high school and everything?"

"I don't think I want to live here, but I don't really know. I've never been anywhere else. I just know it's going to be different, and as much as I complain about this place, I know I'm going to miss it."

She looked at my face, and then looked down again. "And I know I'll miss you too. Brothers and sisters stay close to each other, but cousins grow apart as they get older. Look at our dads. They're brothers and they do everything together, but do they ever talk about their cousins?"

"That doesn't mean we can't stay close!"

"It just happens. It already has, you know. We aren't like we used to be." She said this all in such a clear and strong voice that I couldn't argue. "So, anyway, I just thought I would like to spend this time together. One last big memory we would never be able to forget. Plus, now you really owe me big." She grinned.

"I still don't get why you just didn't quit when Mrs. Nelson told you."

"I think I just wanted to see it all work out. I wanted to see you succeed. You deserve to now."

She sounded so grown-up, but I could still see in her the little girl in ponytails getting off the bus. The sky was a burning red now, and it shone against her dark hair and sun-browned skin. She was so beautiful and I loved her. As she sat drawing on the ground, I could see the dirt underneath her fingernails. She was wearing an old sweatshirt she hated that her dad had gotten from a thrift store.

"Amy, I, I really will always remember this, but it's no use. We're more than four hundred boxes short just to clear the $8,000, and the apples are already falling off the trees. Haven't you heard the thumps?"

"I heard something, but I wasn't sure what it was. So that's it, then? We're just going to stop? We just give all the money to Mrs. Nelson and that's the end?"

"I don't know what else we can do."

"What if everyone just picks? We'll get our parents to help too. I'll convince them."

"I don't think they would, and I don't think there's time."

"Well, then, let's just keep the money and not give it to Mrs. Nelson. Or tell her we only made $1,000 or even $2,000."

"I don't know. Maybe she would sue us or something. Tommy probably knows how many boxes we've sold. He pays attention to things like that."

Amy started chewing her thumbnail like she always did when she was thinking hard. I knew she was considering a confrontation with Mrs. Nelson.

"Do the rest of them know?" I asked. "Sam, Michael, and my sisters?"

"No, I never told them. It's your secret. It's up to you to say something."

All the sick feelings came back. I remembered Michael's skinny body shivering after being drenched with the hose and Sam spitting the taste of Diazinon out of his mouth. I could see Jennifer asleep in the dirt with the lamp at her side.

"Ahhh!" I yelled, and pounded the ground again with my fist. "Why was I so stupid? Why did I agree to this?"

Chapter 16
THE LAST DAY

I stared up at the sky and watched the thin clouds drifting apart in the sunset. Now that I had stopped moving, numbing exhaustion wrapped itself around me. My arms and legs felt like they were growing into the ground. My eyelids sagged shut.

I was jolted awake by the slamming of car doors and voices. I sat up and Amy was still sitting calmly in front of me.

"What's that?" I asked, looking around wildly.

"I don't know," she said, turning her head slowly.

In the distance I could see figures moving in the orchard, dozens of them.

"Someone's in the orchard," I whispered loudly.

"Sam and Michael and the girls probably," said Amy.

"No, there's too many of them." I got to my feet, and my legs felt weak beneath me. The figures were getting closer, and I could see they were carrying ladders. They were calling to each other loudly, but I couldn't understand what they were saying. It wasn't English, more like Spanish. When they were close enough to see their faces, I didn't recognize any of them. They gathered around where Amy and I were sitting and set up their ladders next to the surrounding trees. Without saying anything to us, they started picking apples with very quick hands.

I looked at Amy, who had stood up. She looked as shocked as I was. From the darkening edge of the orchard, I saw another figure moving toward us. It moved slowly and alone. A hundred feet away I recognized Brother Brown. I dropped my picking bag and stumbled toward him. He stopped when he saw me and waited for me to get within earshot.

"Thought you might use a little help," he said in his raspy voice.

I looked at him not sure whether he was some sort of dream. I opened my mouth to speak, but no words came out.

"I hired this outfit through tomorrow. They finished

up at my place a little early so I hope you still have a few trees left for 'em." He smiled with his whole mouth.

"I . . . How did . . . I don't . . ." My throat swelled up, blocking the words.

"I know. I know," he said in an almost tender voice. "Just put out any boxes you have left to fill and they can finish 'em off tomorrow." He took a last long look at me. "And get some sleep, would you." He turned and drifted off into the darkness.

I dropped to my knees. All the tears I had wanted to cry in the dark the weeks before came flooding out of me. I covered my face with my hands and sobbed until my face was streaked with teary mud. I rocked back and forth as all the pain and worry seemed to seep out of me. I felt something touch my shoulder and turned to see Amy standing next to me. I jumped up without even wiping my eyes and ran back to where the workers had their ladders.

I ran up to the first worker I came to and yelled at him, "Thank you! Thank you for helping!"

I got an embarrassed look in return. *"Gracias!"* I shouted.

The man gave a little nod and kept on picking.

I ran from ladder to ladder shouting "Thank you" and *"Gracias."* When I stopped to watch them pick, it was the most amazing thing I had ever seen. Their hands and arms seemed to move effortlessly and automatically, three times as fast as mine. I would have sworn they were angels.

As they filled up their picking bags, the workers moved to the empty boxes set out beside the trees. When they saw the labels of ORANGES and PEARS, they looked at me as if to say, "Is this really right?" I nodded and motioned for them to go ahead and fill them up.

All the empty boxes we had scattered around the trees were quickly filled, and the crew left their ladders and picking bags and walked toward their cars and trucks, which were parked next to the orchard. The last one to leave turned to me and said, *"Mañana."*

I nodded my head and said, *"Gracias."*

Amy and I ran and quickly told the younger kids what was happening. They were closing up the station wagon after loading up a few unsold boxes.

"So let's get this tractor back and load up the rest of those empty boxes and get them out to the orchard. I need everyone's help because it has to be done before tomorrow," I said after explaining the situation.

"Are they really going to be able to fill all the rest in one day?" Sam asked in awe.

"Those guys can probably do it in a few hours," I replied.

Amy nodded her head in agreement.

A new wave of energy swept over me after we ate a little dinner. Michael and Jennifer held flashlights as we loaded up boxes and then dumped them among the un-picked trees. I was glad we had saved the new boxes until the end and felt proud to be able to spread them around. I was in bed by 10:30 and never slept better.

———————

The next day was a Friday, and my mom had to roll me out of bed. I hurried out of the house in my pajamas to check if the workers were back in the orchard but saw no one. On the way to the bus stop, the orchard was still empty.

"Amy, there were people out in the orchard helping us last night, right? We put all the rest of the boxes out?" I asked.

"Yes! Why are you asking that?"

"I just want to make sure it was all real and I wasn't dreaming."

I watched the orchard drift past as the bus pulled away. All day at school, I thought about those empty boxes and whether they would be full when I arrived home. I tried to think of a good excuse so I could go to the school's office and call my mom and ask her to look outside. My brain was too numb to think of anything creative, though, so I spent the day sitting and wonder-ing.

On the bus ride home, I figured that even if Brother Brown's work crew had shown up right after we had left in the morning, they would still only have seven hours before our return. I had told Sam they could easily do the whole job in just a few hours, but now I wasn't so sure. As the bus got closer to the orchard, I could see it was empty of people. My heart started beating fast. Could they really have finished already, or had they never showed up? I jumped out of the bus and sprinted into the orchard toward where we had left the boxes the night before. I tore the lid off the first one I came to.

It was full of apples.

I checked three or four more just to be sure and then gave a loud yell and danced around the boxes. It felt like Christmas morning in some rich family's house. My cousins and sisters had followed me from the bus stop and found me still skipping around the boxes.

"So I guess they're all full?" asked Amy, grinning.

"Now all we have to do is sell them," I said. "That's the easy part."

"Says you!" Lisa responded defensively.

"Amy, how about you try to do some selling with everyone else, and Sam and I can stack up these boxes," I said as everyone began to separate.

"Okay, but only because you're not good with people," she called out to me.

Sam and I spent the rest of the day hauling the remaining four hundred–plus full boxes to the end of the rows and stacking them three high. We figured this would make it easier to load them on the wagon for the trip up to the road. When we were done, I was amazed that Sam had handled the previous six hundred by himself without complaining.

"Sam, your back must be made of steel," I told him, trying to stretch out the strains and pulls in my own back.

"You'll get used to it," he said, as if I had never seen a box of apples before.

We walked up to the station wagon to check on the others. I was glad to see Amy trying to convince an older couple to buy a bushel.

"How long do you think it will take you to sell four hundred more boxes?" I asked Lisa.

"I think tomorrow will be the biggest day of the year," she replied.

"Why tomorrow?"

"Everyone who's been stopping talks about the Navajo Fair tomorrow. There's going to be tons of cars going by."

The Navajo Fair was a yearly celebration that involved parades, powwows, and various other events in Shiprock. Shiprock was west of Fruitland about the same distance away from us as Farmington, but in the opposite direction. Shiprock was on the Navajo reservation and had very few stores, so most people living there would drive to Farmington to shop. During the fair, the extra visitors filled Highway 550 with traffic, and we were right in the middle.

"Should we make some special signs or something?" I asked Lisa.

"I think we should put some of us on the other side of the road. That way we can get them coming and going." Lisa spoke as if she had been doing this sort of thing for years. "We can take one of these banners over there too," she continued, pointing at the signs she had made.

———————⌐

By eight o'clock the next morning, Lisa and Jennifer were positioned at the station wagon with fifty full boxes stacked next to it. On the other side of the road were Amy and Michael. There were no old cars available for them to sit in, so we set up an old pup tent we used whenever we went camping. Another fifty boxes sat next to it.

Sam and I were going to work on bringing out the rest of the apples throughout the day and also help both sides of the road with selling. I could tell Lisa viewed the whole thing as a competition and wanted me to keep careful track of how many boxes went to each side. She had given Amy an empty peanut butter jar to put money in and had included a little change and carefully labeled the amount on the outside.

The morning started off slowly, and I decided to

wander across the road to help Amy and Michael. The first customer I talked with pulled up in a beat-up Ford pickup.

"You got any of them white apples?" called the old Navajo woman in the passenger seat.

"No, but we have some really good red ones. You can try 'em," I said.

I ran and got a good-size apple and wiped it on my shirt until it was nice and shiny. The old woman took the apple and without trying it said, "We wanted the white ones," and they drove off.

It took me several attempts to sell my first box. Finally, a Navajo man gave me a $10 bill and then kicked his foot at one of the boxes. "This one," he said roughly.

"Okay, thanks," I replied, taking the money and handing him his change.

He kept looking at the box, then at me. I finally realized he wanted me to carry it to his truck. I was going to tell him to do it himself, but I looked across the road and saw Lisa and Jennifer carrying a box to a truck while a man looked on. They each were holding one side of the box and struggling to get it over the tailgate. I grudgingly grabbed the box and threw it in the man's truck.

We discovered after a few hours that Lisa's side of the road had a distinct advantage. There were many more cars heading to Farmington in the morning, and so she would often have five or six cars at a time pulled off beside her. She had unloaded her first fifty boxes by 11:00 a.m. and had a satisfied look on her face.

On the other side of the road, Michael was doing his best to keep Amy and me distracted. He started rolling apples onto the pavement as cars would drive by, trying to time his rolls so that the apples would be smashed underneath a tire.

"What are you doing?" I yelled.

"We do this all the time when I help Sam bring the apples up," he said coolly.

"I was wondering where all those stains on the road were coming from," said Amy. "I knew there couldn't be that much roadkill."

I restrained myself from telling Michael to stop since I wanted to keep everyone happy.

"So what else do you do to entertain yourself up here at the road?" I asked him.

"The best thing that ever happened was when the Hostess Bakery truck came along, and we traded him a box of apples for a whole tray of day-old pies. You know the kind that come by themselves wrapped up in a little package," Michael said, thinking about it happily.

"How come me and Jackson never got any pies?" asked Amy angrily.

"Well, we decided if we didn't tell you, you wouldn't miss them."

In the afternoon the traffic pattern began to switch,

and there were more people headed back toward Ship-rock. Long lines of cars pulled off both sides of the road, some of them trying each side to find the best deal. Sam and I stayed busy bringing more boxes up from the or-chard, which I was much happier doing than trying to sell.

In the evening the traffic pattern had completely switched, and Amy's side of the road was swamped while Lisa sat around nervously. She insisted that we load all the remaining boxes of apples onto the wagon and park it on the other side of the highway, about one hundred feet from Amy.

The final boxes and bags were sold in a blur of activity as a seemingly endless stream of cars and trucks moved toward Shiprock. Right around 7:00 p.m., Sam carried the last full box to a waiting pickup and it was over.

"We're all out!" Amy shouted to cars that kept pulling off the road. "You have to wait till next year."

"Michael, pull down that sign so people don't stop anymore," I yelled to him.

We yanked up the pup tent, threw everything onto the wagon, and forced the tractor through the traffic and across the highway toward home. Lisa grabbed Amy's jar of money and went into her room and shut the door. Everyone else stood outside pacing around and talking nervously. I bit my lip and stared at my feet, hardly dar-ing to think about what was going on behind the door.

Lisa reappeared after about half an hour. "I'm done counting; everyone can come in," she said, trying to sound very important. We all squeezed into her room, and I sat on her bed next to Amy. Lisa had lined up at least a dozen jars full of money on her floor. She held up a spiral notebook, where she had kept track of numbers and dates.

"Okay, I first want to announce today's results. My team had a total of $116 more than Amy's," she said, with a proud grin.

"What are you talking about?" asked Amy, who sounded annoyed. "I didn't even know you were keeping track of that. Your side of the road was better, anyway."

"Okay, okay, let's not argue about that," I said, laughing uncomfortably. "We were all helping each other, so I don't think it matters. What we care most about are the totals."

Lisa flipped a page in her book very officially. "Today was by far our biggest day," she began.

"We know, we know! Just tell us the numbers," said Michael impatiently.

"Today's total was $3,518," she barked out.

Everyone's eyes opened wide in appreciation.

"And the grand total?" I asked.

"We made $9,180. Plus thirty cents."

I had a feeling I would remember that number for

the rest of my life. Everyone looked at each other as if a rocket had just gone off.

"We're so rich!" yelled Michael.

"Now we just have to figure out all our shares," said Lisa excitedly.

I didn't say anything to interrupt their celebration, and I kept the same wide smile on my face. I looked over at Amy. She was smiling happily, too, but in her eyes I could see a look that said, "I'm glad it's you who has to tell them and not me."

Chapter 17
Bags of Cash and Secret Envelopes

The celebration in Lisa's room continued for another hour or so. By the end, nearly everyone was delirious from a combination of newfound riches and physical exhaustion. Michael had decided we should all pool our money and buy a boat that we could go up and down the river on. None of the girls seemed interested in this idea, so he spent most of the time trying to convince Sam and me how fun it would be.

At the same time, Lisa was making plans to use all the money to build a snow-cone stand up at the road. "We could really clean up. This apple money is nothing compared to snow cones," she kept saying.

I let them talk themselves out before I spoke up. "Before we can spend anything, though, I need to pay off our bills and give Mrs. Nelson her part," I said to disappointed faces.

"Why don't you do it now?" asked Michael.

"I want to go to the bank and trade in some of these smaller bills," I said. I also wanted someone else to count it all, but I didn't dare tell Lisa that. "I've got to try and convince Mom to take me when they're open."

"Jennifer and I can help you ask her," Lisa volunteered.

"Okay, but I think we better keep this all to ourselves until everything is settled. Don't even tell our parents how much we made," I said, trying to sound very secretive.

"Good idea," agreed Michael in a loud whisper. "They might try to take it all for themselves."

"So just give me a few days to get everything straightened out," I concluded.

"You got it," Michael whispered again. I had the feeling, however, that he would be bugging me constantly until he got some money.

———————⊣

The next day I saw Brother Brown in Sunday school. He gave a lesson on the Good Samaritan, and it sounded very deep and almost emotional. I was trying to figure out what he was doing differently that day when I turned to look at everyone else in the class. They were all looking down or out the window as usual. I glared around the room. When Brother Brown paused a little in what he was saying, I spoke up loudly, "Hey, why aren't you guys paying attention?"

The other kids in the class flinched. Instead of looking at Brother Brown, though, they spent the rest of the time staring at me.

When it was over, I hung around again until the other kids had gone.

"I don't know how to thank you for everything. I couldn't have done any of it without your help," I said, looking at him.

He kept his head down and stared at his shoes. "Don't mention it," he mumbled.

"If you ever need any kind of help from me, just ask. I don't really know much about anything, but I'm willing to try and work hard."

He kept looking down and moved toward the door. As he brushed past me, he stopped and grabbed my arm right under the shoulder. He gave me an awkward shake and then kept walking. I felt a kind of electricity shoot through my body as he touched me with his weathered hand.

"See you next week," I called after him.

After church my sisters and I worked on my mom until she agreed to take me to the bank in Farmington after school the next day. Lisa volunteered to come too, but I told her she better not neglect her homework and extra reading anymore. She readily agreed.

I had Lisa put all the money into little brown paper bags grouped by denomination. She found some rubber bands and counted out groups of $100 and put the rubber bands around them. The little bags were then placed in a big grocery bag. We kept all the quarters, dimes, and nickels we had in a large jar, and I put that in a grocery bag too.

———————→

I hurried my mom out the door as fast as I could on Monday so I would have as much time as possible at the bank. We rode in silence, and she didn't ask what was inside my bags. She dropped me off at Citizens Bank at four o'clock and said she would be at the supermarket and would pick me back up at five.

I walked uneasily into the bank and stood in a short line of people waiting to see tellers, holding the money very close to me. There were four tellers helping people and three people in front of me. I looked over the tellers nervously, trying to guess which one would end up helping me. By the time I got to the front of the line, I had gotten a good look at all of them except the one on my far right. A large man was standing in front of that spot, blocking my view. He moved away suddenly and I heard a female voice call, "Next, please."

I moved cautiously to my right and got my first look at the face behind the voice. She was young and very pretty, with bright green eyes and golden brown hair. I could feel myself turning red as I moved more slowly toward her.

"What can I do for you today?" she said smiling.

"I uh . . . uh . . ." I kept staring at her teeth, which were very white and straight.

"Do you have something in the bag you need help with?"

"It's money," I said obviously. "I was hoping to get it counted and change it for some larger bills."

"That sounds easy enough. How much do you have?"

I didn't really want to say, so I started pulling out the little sacks that had been marked with the kind of bills they contained. The teller looked inside a few very cautiously.

"Wow, there's quite a bit here. Where did you get all this?"

She asked in such a friendly and sincere way, I felt that it was best to explain the whole story. I left out select parts like the manure and the dump boxes, but painted a pretty complete picture of the rest. She made for a good audience, too, even looking amazed at certain parts of my explanation.

"We better get counting, then, if we're going to finish by tomorrow," she said. "Let's start with the biggest bills."

The biggest bills we had were twenties, and she grabbed them all and piled them into a stack while counting. She wrote a number down and moved on to the tens. Her hands flew as she counted, and her lips moved very fast whispering out numbers. I peeked over at them shyly, amazed at how red they looked against her white teeth.

She made good progress until she came to all the dollar bills. I began to wish that Lisa had given more of those as change to people. The teller counted over fifteen hundred of them, and the clock hit five even before she was done. All the other customers were gone, and the rest of the bank employees were starting to leave.

"Do you have to go?" I asked when she finished with the dollars.

"I can finish up," she said happily.

"I'm sorry it's so much counting."

"That's okay. I'm kind of interested to find out how much is here."

When she looked at the jar of change, she squinted and said, "We might need some help on that one."

She took the jar and poured it into a shiny machine that did all the counting and separated the coins. She wrote down the total and came back to me. She added up some more numbers, wrote it on a piece of paper, and then held it close to her.

"Are you ready for the total?"

"Yes," I said slowly.

"It's $9,180.30."

I was amazed both to hear her say such a large number and that Lisa had been exactly right.

"That's about what I thought," I said, trying to react calmly.

"Would you like to deposit that into an account or maybe get a cashier's check?"

I felt dumb asking what a cashier's check was, so I just said, "Can I just get it in large bills?"

"Whatever you want. Just hope you don't lose them. Do you want hundreds?"

"Can I get $8,000 in hundreds and the rest in twenties and tens?"

She counted out the money and then said, "Let me get you an envelope or two for that."

She brought over some manila envelopes, and we slid the money inside. I noticed for the first time that she wore a small nametag that read KELLY. I felt kind of nervous using her name but said, "Thank you so much for your help, Kelly. I'm glad I got your window."

"My pleasure," she said smiling.

"Can I ask you one more thing? Do you know where I can get a document copied?"

She looked around. "If it's just a page, I can copy it for you."

I reached into one of the paper sacks and pulled out the piece of paper I had gotten from the lawyer's office with Mrs. Nelson. Kelly looked it over curiously and then went over to a copy machine. She came back a few minutes later.

"I think this was a copy, so now you have a copy of a copy and it doesn't look that great," she said.

"That's okay. It'll be good enough."

I thanked her repeatedly as she walked me to the door of the bank. As I turned to say goodbye, I wished I had more money to count. I tried to wave at her again through the glass doors, but she had already walked away.

My mom was sitting in her car waiting for me in the parking lot. "What took so long in there? Where's the money from the grocery bags?"

It had to be obvious why I needed the bank, even if she hadn't brought it up earlier. "There was a line to begin with," I replied, "and . . . I'll explain later." I wanted to tell her all about Kelly and the money counting, but I stopped myself and hoped she wouldn't press for details.

"Okay. It's your secret little project. I just hope your father doesn't beat us home."

I ran into my room when we arrived before Lisa or Jennifer could stop me. I closed the door and hid the envelopes of money deep in my closet. All I said to Lisa that night was "You were exactly right about the total." She was so happy with herself that she didn't ask about anything else.

———————⟩

The next day after school, I grabbed the envelope full of tens and twenties and knocked on my cousins' door. Sam answered.

"Wanna go for a ride?" I asked.

He walked out the door before asking, "Where to?"

We climbed on the tractor, and I let him drive to General Supply. I put the envelope down my shirt so it wouldn't blow out of my hands.

We walked through the doors, and I was surprised to see Jimmy behind the counter.

"I thought you only worked during the summer," I said, walking up to him.

"After school too, remember?" he replied. "You ever get those boxes?"

"Yep, and we just finished selling them all," I told him proudly. "Thought I should come and pay the bill."

Jimmy went and got the card he usually wrote our charges on and started adding things up.

"You owe $534," he said when he was done.

"Wow, how much for each thing?" I asked.

"It was $300 for the boxes, almost a couple hundred for the poison, rolls of plastic, cans of pop—it adds up."

I reached into the envelope and handed him the money and then watched as he crossed off all the items on the card.

"Do you think you could start a fresh card for my dad, with none of those things written on it?" I asked him.

He looked at me, smiled, and tore up the card. "Sure," he said.

"And can I get a receipt for all that stuff? Actually can I get two copies for my records?"

He shook his head, teasing me, but wrote out the receipts I wanted.

"Thanks, Jimmy," I said as we walked off. "You working next summer?"

"We'll see," he called out.

When Sam and I got home, I said to him, "Can you ask Amy to come over and talk to me in a couple of hours?"

I went into my room and started writing a letter to Mrs. Nelson. I had a feeling that she wouldn't answer her door and talk to me, but I hoped she would read a letter. I tried to explain in it that I had lived up to my part of our deal and that I was putting the $8,000 into an envelope with the letter, along with a copy of the agreement and a receipt for the supplies we used. I also wrote about how much I learned and how much I appreciated her believing that I could do it. I promised to take care of the orchard too.

When Amy came over, I took her into my room and let her read the letter.

"What do you think?" I asked when she had finished.

"Sounds pretty good. Do you think it will convince her?"

"I don't know. Would it convince you?"

"I'm not crazy in the first place. Let's see the money."

I pulled out the envelope full of hundreds and handed it to her.

"Whoa!" she said as her eyes widened. "I don't think I've ever seen a hundred before." She spread the money on my bed, running her hands over the top of it. A strange look came over her face. "Let's just keep it!" she said. "With our share, we could both buy cars! Cool ones!"

I bit my lip. "I'm afraid to." I could feel heat rising on the top of my head. "I've got to keep my part of deal," I said.

"Okay, I know," she said, looking a little embarrassed.

"So can you come with me tomorrow to give this to her? I want you there as a witness so no one can say we didn't give her the money."

"Let's do it right after school, then," she said.

I didn't sleep well that night. I kept going over the first conversations I had with Mrs. Nelson and our trip to the lawyer's office. It all seemed so long ago.

———————⌐

After school on Wednesday, I stuffed the money and papers into the manila envelope Kelly had given me. I sealed it, wrote Mrs. Nelson's name on it, and headed over to get Amy.

I met Lisa in the kitchen. "What are you doing? What's that?" she asked, pointing to the envelope.

"Business," I said, and hurried away before she could ask any more questions.

Amy and I stood on Mrs. Nelson's porch and looked at each other. I was thinking hard about what to say in case she answered the door.

"Go ahead," said Amy pointing at the doorbell.

I let out a sigh, reached over, and pressed it. We could hear the chimes inside but nothing else. After half a minute, I looked over at Amy.

"She's got to be in there," Amy said loudly. "Her car's right out front." She pounded on the door. When that didn't work, she pounded again while yelling, "Open up, we know you're there!"

I pulled her hand away from the door. "That's just going to make her mad," I whispered.

"So what?" she spit out. After calming down a little, she asked, "Now what should we do?"

"What if we just leave it?" I suggested.

We couldn't think of anything better to do, so we jammed the envelope full of money into the crack of the door. It was hard to walk away from it, especially after Amy reminded me it would buy a nice new car, but we eventually backed off the porch while keeping our eyes on the door.

"What if she just takes it and never says anything?" Amy asked.

"I guess then we'll have to tell our parents," I said, dreading the possibility. "But you're a witness. And Lisa knew exactly how much money there was, and so did the woman at the bank. I'm going to keep an eye on the door from the orchard. Besides, we forgot to take some apples down to the Wheelers, so I'm going to try and pick some."

We returned home, and I grabbed some cardboard boxes my dad had brought home from work. They weren't fruit boxes and were an odd shape so we hadn't used them before, but I didn't think the Wheelers would mind. I kept my eye on the envelope as much as possible, which was still visible in the door. The weather had turned colder, and I could see my breath if I blew hard enough. I moved up and down several rows trying to find enough good apples to fill the Wheelers' boxes. Without the pressure I had felt just a few days earlier, I realized that I recognized the features of individual trees and could even remember picking and spraying certain ones. I even had my favorites—the trees that produced fat, low-hanging apples. It seemed silly to name them, but I had studied them so closely, I could recognize them by sight.

I finished with the boxes and then sat in a spot secluded in the orchard where I could keep an eye on the envelope and door. There was no movement, and eventually I had to stand and pace back and forth to keep warm. Darkness settled in and I couldn't see the door anymore, so I reluctantly returned home.

———⌐

The next day on the way to the bus stop, I could see the envelope still there. I looked over at Amy with a worried expression. She shrugged her shoulders knowingly. I thought about running and getting the envelope and hiding it back in my room, but just kept moving toward the bus.

School seemed to last much longer that day. I squeezed out of the bus in the afternoon with an urge to run and check the envelope, but walked coolly next to Amy instead. We made it halfway down the dirt road wordlessly until the door came into view. The envelope was gone.

I gulped and stopped walking. "Now you just have to wait and see what she does," said Amy, trying to sound reassuring.

To take my mind off the envelope, Sam and I drove down to the Wheelers' to deliver the apples I had picked.

Jerry was more excited than ever to see us, and grabbed an apple and bit into it without wiping it off or washing his hands.

"Delicious!" he said enthusiastically. "What's your secret, boys?"

"Lots of fertilizer," I said, smiling.

"That's got to be it. This place only makes the best." He laughed.

Sam and I carried the boxes over to the building Jerry always came out of. "This has to be the sweetest trade I've ever made," he kept saying. I had the feeling as we drove off that he would have liked us to stay the rest of the day.

———⟩

Despite the cold, I kept watching Mrs. Nelson's house from the orchard. Nothing happened for the rest of the week, and I couldn't even see any movement through her windows. I decided on Monday afternoon that I might as well fill up some boxes with apples for my mom and aunt before they all fell to the ground. I grabbed more of my dad's non-fruit boxes and went to work. I was able to keep an eye on Mrs. Nelson's since picking had almost become automatic and I could do it mostly by feel.

A couple of hours after I started, Tommy's car pulled up to his mom's house. He went inside, and then a few minutes later started walking down the dirt lane to my house. He saw me in the orchard and headed toward me. As he got closer, I moved down the ladder I was on and stood clutching it with one hand. I thought of running to get Amy. I hated to be alone if he was going to confront me.

Tommy reached my ladder, huffing loudly with his breath visible in the cold air. "Back out here, huh?" he began.

"Thought I'd pick a few of the leftovers for my family before they drop."

"Well, might as well go ahead and give you this," he said, and pulled a manila envelope out of his coat pocket.

At first I thought it was the envelope I had left on Mrs. Nelson's doorstep, but then I saw it had different writing on it. I took it from his gloved hands.

"Go ahead and open it," he said.

"What is it?" I asked as I turned over the flap on top of the envelope. I pulled out the papers inside. They looked like legal documents or something, and I could see numbers written on them.

"It's the deed to the orchard."

"It is? What does that mean?" I asked while thumbing through the papers.

He pointed to the last page and said, "That's my mom's signature down there at the bottom. It means all you have to do is sign next to it and the orchard's yours. Everything else has been filed with the county already."

I looked up at him in disbelief. "Really? Aren't you mad about this or something?" I blurted out.

"Me? Why should I be mad?"

"Wasn't it supposed to go to you?"

"Maybe when my mom dies, but she'll probably out-live me just to prove a point. Actually, I'm kind of glad it's going to be yours. Then she can't keep nagging me about it."

I stared back down at the documents. "Well, is she mad?" I asked him.

"I don't know about mad. Maybe a little embarrassed and feeling silly. I'm sure she'll get over it next spring when the trees are blooming." He said this last part try-ing to imitate her voice.

"You know when she told me about your little agree-ment," Tommy continued, "I mostly felt sorry for you. My mom has no idea what it takes to make any money doing something like this. That $8,000 sounded impos-sible to me. I didn't want to tell you that because you looked so eager that I hated to discourage you."

"What did you think was going to happen?"

"I thought you would just kind of give up. When I saw the $8,000, I was floored. At first my mom wanted to think of a way not to turn over the orchard, but I kept telling her she'd be the laughingstock of the whole state if people found out she cheated some kid. I figured she owed it to you, no matter how cuckoo the agreement was. Of course, the only thing that really worked on her was threatening to stop coming out to see her."

"Thanks," I said, although it didn't sound like enough.

"And by the way, I made her sign over the water rights too. This place isn't much good without them."

I didn't really know what water rights were, but I figured they must have something to do with the canal.

"Thanks again, Tommy. How about the other stuff, like the ladders?"

"Go ahead and keep them. She's not gonna need them for anything."

He looked down at my hands that were still holding the envelope and then looked around the orchard. "So how'd you do it?" he asked. "I mean, that's a lot of apples."

I thought hard about his question and about everything that had fallen into place over the past eight months—the library book, my cousins and sisters, the old Ford tractor, the apples not freezing, Brother Brown, Jimmy, the free boxes at the dump. Take away one of those things, and we probably would have failed.

"I guess I was pretty lucky."

"Whatever it was, I'll always be impressed," replied Tommy, nodding his head.

I looked down at the envelope, and it suddenly felt heavy. Tommy deserved some of the credit too. "If you didn't stand up for me, well, I don't know what . . ." I trailed off.

Tommy shuffled his feet and looked at the ground. "Ahhh, I figured I owed it to my dad. I never did help him like I probably should have. I dunno, I guess I regret what he probably thought of me, how we never seemed to have anything in common. If I plowed up these trees, he'd probably haunt me forever. It's better having you worry about them."

Tommy held his hands up to his ears like he was trying to keep them warm. "I gotta run, before I freeze." He turned and started walking away. "Hey, Jackson," he called, "just don't turn it into a trailer park, okay? You'd make me look like a moron."

"Don't worry," I shouted. "You want some of these apples?"

"Nah," he yelled back without turning around. "I'll catch you next year."

Chapter 18
BREAKING UP AND STARTING OVER

In a way, it felt unsatisfying that the paper I was holding was what made me the owner of the orchard. I looked through the pages, and there were words about land and plots but nothing about the trees. As I looked at them in their shadowy rows standing above me, I didn't feel like I owned them. Maybe it felt a little more like responsibility, which had come over me very gradually. I told myself it was what Mrs. Nelson wanted all along, if she was ever really serious about that "true heir" stuff.

That night I went over and told Amy and showed her the papers. She looked over them and then looked up at me very proudly. "Well, how do you feel? This is just what you've been hoping for and tricking us all into."

"I don't know. Now that it's real, it feels a little weird."

"Have you told your other employees yet?"

"No, so please don't say anything. They've been bugging me non-stop about the money, but I've got to give it a few days to let it sink in and to make sure no one over there changes their minds." I gestured toward Mrs. Nelson's house. "I also have to figure out what I'm going to say."

———⌐

It took all the way until the next Monday for me to get up the nerve to talk to the younger kids. I asked everyone, including Amy, to come to my room after dinner so we could discuss something important. They all sat on my floor expectantly while I sat on my bed.

"I just want to start by saying you all were better workers than I ever hoped for. If you didn't know it, I had no idea what I was doing and just kind of made things up as we went along," I said.

"Oh, we knew it," said Amy.

"Yeah, yeah. Well, if you remember how this whole thing got started, I was talking to Mrs. Nelson one day and she wanted to share the money that could be made from the orchard. But I left out some of the details that I have to tell you now."

"Oh, really?" said Lisa. "Isn't it a little late to be telling us now?"

Everyone stared at me with a mixture of fear and disgust. I went ahead with the whole story, including the trip to the lawyer's office, the envelope with the $8,000 in it, and then the conversation I had with Tommy. I held up the deed as a kind of proof of what I was saying. I told them how at first I had hoped to make a lot more than the $8,000 and planned to give all the extra to them. No one said a word the whole time. They just sat there with their mouths open. Michael was the first out of the gate with a response.

"How could you be so stupid?" he spit out, shaking his head. "That money was ours too. What makes you think you could just take it all and give it away without even asking us?"

"Yeah, we should have voted or something," said Lisa. "Except you knew we wouldn't have voted to do that."

I looked over at Amy for some support, but she just looked away.

"I know. I know I was stupid. It's just that I signed the agreement, and I was afraid she was going to take the money, anyway. And I'm sorry I didn't tell you the whole thing up front. I was afraid you wouldn't help, I guess," I said, trying to sound as sorry as possible.

"Yeah right, you're sorry," said Michael.

"Listen, since we agreed on percentages, if you want, you can own a percentage of the orchard."

"That's just a stupid piece of paper," said Michael. "We want the money."

"Okay, how about this. Now that I'm the owner, we don't have to give any money to Mrs. Nelson on anything we earn in the future. What if next year you all get twice the percentages we agreed on this year?"

Lisa's eyes got big, and I realized I should have thought through the numbers before making the offer.

"You're trying to trick us again, aren't you?" said Michael angrily. He was looking back and forth between me and Lisa.

"Actually, that's a better deal than we had if we make the same amount of money next year," said Lisa in a calculating tone. "If we make $9,000 again and I get twenty percent, that's $1,800 for me. And over $1,600 for you, Michael."

"I want my money now. How are we supposed to trust him a year from now?" demanded Michael.

"We could put it in a contract and write it all up, just like Jackson had," interrupted Jennifer from the corner.

"Yeah, we can have a contract," I said carefully, still trying to add up percentages in my head. "Plus you all can split up the money that's left this year. I won't take any of it."

I brought out the remaining $646.30 and laid it out in front of them. The sight of the cash and the idea of the contract seemed to pacify them. They held a vote and it was unanimous in favor of the plan, although Michael kept pointing out that I could be tricking them again.

I also reminded everyone that we had done most of the hard work already. We could probably skip fertilizing the next year, the trees wouldn't need much pruning, and we could even try to hire Brother Brown's work crew for picking. They all seemed to agree, and I was amazed at how short their memories were.

I wrote out a contract right there in pen on a loose-leaf piece of paper. I tried to make it sound as official as possible by including words like "hereby" and "therefore."

Amy said she was "keeping her options open," so she didn't want to be a part of the contract. Everyone else signed their name on the paper. Lisa worked out the math and concluded that I would get 24 percent of next year's profits.

"Twenty-four percent? And he gets the orchard?" protested Michael.

"I'm the oldest. I'm supposed to get the most."

That reminder of our original logic stopped him grudgingly in his tracks.

"And I'm not going to take anything this year," I added.

...RYONE'S PERCENTAGE OF PROFITS
NEXT YEAR

Jennifer 16%
Michael 18%
Lisa 20%
Sam 22%
Jackson 24%
_____
Total 100%

"Let's give the contract to someone trustworthy to keep so Jackson can't change it," said Michael. "Amy, you better hold on to it."

"You know, though, you have to work hard or the agreement's off," I said.

"We aren't the ones I'd worry about," said Michael.

We split up the money after the contract signing. It wasn't really according to the percentages we had originally agreed on, but I figured it was close enough. I gave $200 to Amy, which she shoved instantly into her pocket. "I'm also going to give you some of my share next year," I said to her, "no matter if you help or not."

"I'll count on it," she replied with a laugh.

Sam got $142, Lisa $122, Michael $102, and Jennifer $80.30. I reminded them again that I wasn't keeping anything for myself. Holding the money seemed to make them almost pleasant. Soon Lisa had convinced Sam and Jennifer that it wouldn't take much to set up a snow-cone stand next to the apple-selling operation, and she happily added up how much money she'd have by next year. I kept reminding her that her percentage of apple money was after expenses, which might include paying for some temporary pickers. Nothing I said slowed her runaway calculations.

When the meeting finally ended, I decided it had gone far better than I deserved. They had started off ready to kill me, and I ended up with a signed work contract for next year.

Amy spent all her money on new clothes the very next day, bringing home six bags crammed with jeans and shirts, doubling her wardrobe. Michael couldn't convince his mom to let him spend his money on pop, so I drove him down to General Supply so he could buy four cases of it. He hid them under his bed along with at least a hundred candy bars. He also bought three pocketknives and a half-dozen baby chicks before I convinced him he couldn't hold down anything more in the wagon without it flying off. Everyone else saved most of their money and, under Lisa's direction, opened savings accounts at the bank.

When I finally revealed the whole story to my parents,

couldn't decide whether she was proud or an-
y. "Why didn't you tell us? I just don't understand it,"
she kept repeating.

Eventually parental pride won out, and she expressed
it by baking about a dozen pies using the last apples I'd
plucked from the trees. By the tenth pie, she'd perfected
the recipe so that the warm crust and apple slices melted
away in your mouth. I got as much as I wanted, plus ice
cream on top.

My dad kept reading over the deed without saying
much, as if he were looking for some kind of mistake. He
finally set it aside and said, shaking his head, "You are one
sneaky kid. How did you ever pull this off?" His voice
had a mixture of pride and awe in it. "Why don't you sell
that place? Someone could probably put three or four
houses on that land. If you could get $10,000 an acre . . ."

"No, no. I can't do that. The trees have to stay," I insisted.

"Whatever you say, farm boy. But since we're neighbors now, you better keep the weeds down on your
place." He chuckled and flashed a proud grin.

"I will if you keep your yard cleaned up," I replied.

As I knew she would, my aunt laughed and laughed
when she found out the whole story and my uncle
started calling me "the apple tycoon." "If you're ever
looking for a replacement for Michael, give me a call,"
he teased.

In some ways, Amy was right about what would happen between us sooner than I ever expected. After the apples were picked, she stopped taking the bus and would instead ride with friends who could drive to school. She also got a serious boyfriend she was always talking to or hanging out with. I hated his guts but didn't dare say so to him or Amy.

I watched her go, feeling more helpless than I ever had surrounded by three hundred wild apple trees. I dreaded her growing up and looking at me differently. Inside I promised that when I thought of her, I would always begin with a scene from somewhere in that orchard. She'd have sunburned cheeks and muddy fingernails. She'd be that same little girl I waited for at the bus stop, her eyes shining in the New Mexico sun.

———————

She wasn't with Sam, Michael, and me that next February as we dragged the ladders over the frozen ground. We forgot the radio, so it was quiet when we made our first cuts with the pruning scissors. Beneath its dark winter skin, the wood was soft and alive, as if the trees were expecting us, expecting spring.

"Just think how easy it's going to be, now that we know what we're doing," I sang out.

Sam snipped away diligently on the second ladder.

Michael was already talking about how good the Shasta I promised him was going to taste.

ACKNOWLEDGMENTS

Thanks to everyone who read and made
suggestions when this was still in a raw form:
Amanda K., Amy T., Carly S., Catherine S.,
Heather N., Jennifer P., Lisa S., Megan M.,
Ross M., and Sara M.

And special thanks to my super-agent,
Emily Sylvan Kim, and my editor, Ann Rider.
Their guidance and vision made this
more than just a dream.

Aaron Hawkins tended his family's orchard as a child on a New Mexican plateau. He graduated from the California Institute of Technology with a bachelor's of science in applied physics and from UC Santa Barbara with a Ph.D. in electrical and computer engineering. He is now a professor of electrical engineering at Brigham Young University, as well as the author of *The Handbook of Optofluidics*. He was inspired to write this, his first novel, from his memories of the family orchard. "I was never really paid for any of the work," he writes, "but looking back, I think of it as transformative. I hoped to create a story that contained some of the things I learned—appreciation for nature and growing something, the self-esteem that comes from hard work, and the love for family and friends that comes from struggling together." He lives with his wife and kids in Provo, Utah.

WWW.AARONHAWKINS.COM